From the screenwriter
of *Angels in the Outfield*
comes...

KEEPER

BY

HOLLY GOLDBERG SLOAN

www.scobre.com

Scobre Press Corporation
2255 Calle Clara
La Jolla, CA 92037

Scobre Press books may be purchased
for educational, business or sales
promotional use.

First Scobre edition published 2002.

Edited by Ramey Temple & Michael Fisher
Cover Art by Anne Herlihy & Ralph King
Cover Layout by Michael Lynch

ISBN 0-9741695-8-7

www.scobre.com

To all the dreamers...

We at Scobre Press are proud to bring you another book in our "Dream Series." In case this is your first Scobre book, here's what we're all about: The goal of Scobre is to influence young people by entertaining them with books about athletes who act as role models. The moral dilemmas facing the athletes in a Scobre story run parallel to situations facing many young people today. After reading a Scobre book, our hope is that young people will be able to respond to adversity in their lives in the same heroic fashion as the athletes depicted in our books.

This book is about Sasha Lewis, a young girl whose fear of everything forces her to live her life without taking any risks. But after her best friend tricks her into joining the soccer team, her fears begin to fade, and her dreams begin to form.

We invite you now to come along with us, sit down, get comfortable, and read a book that will dare you to dream. Scobre dedicates this book to all the people who are chasing down their own dreams. We're sure that Sasha will inspire you to reach for the stars.

Here's Sasha, and "Keeper."

To Max and Calvin

ONE

I have a secret. Not the kind of secret like I have about our neighbor Mrs. Higgenlooper. I saw her once in the parking lot at Costco in the way back by the dumpsters. I swear I saw her kissing a man in a blue striped shirt, and he wasn't Mr. Higgenlooper. And not a secret like Jenny Chow wrote nasty things on the wall in the bathroom at school with the edge of a fingernail file. This secret is about me.

I'm afraid of things.

All kinds of people are afraid of spiders and snakes (so it's okay that I'm totally and completely freaked out about those). And some people are afraid to fly or go to movies with skulls on the posters. That's all considered normal. I've got bigger problems.

I'm sort of afraid of everything. Clowns. Big trees. Any room that's dark. Thunder. Firecrackers. Cats. Motorcycles. Bees. Snowballs. Most knives.

Some forks. Car wash places. Elevators. Hamsters. The guys behind the sushi counter who yell when you come in. Certain shades of purple. Alleys. Sprinkler heads. Any dog bigger than a cat and I already explained about the cats. Men in beards. Men in moustaches. Blood. Ketchup (because it looks like blood). And most kinds of cheese. That's just my starter list.

I think you get the picture. It's hard being completely and totally terrorized by a package of string cheese. But think about this: on top of everything, I've got to hide my fears. I've got to hide the fact that twice a day the hair is standing up on my arms and I feel like running from the room screaming. I've got to pretend to be normal. It's a big, big struggle. No wonder I'm tired all the time.

That's why my friend Courtney is so important. She's known me since kindergarten, when I refused to sit by the window. I'm uncomfortable with most heating units and there was an old radiator there. I moved to the seat next to her and that's when we met. She's the kind of person who collects squirrels and baby birds when they fall out of trees. She'll feed them sugar water with eyedroppers in old shoe boxes stuffed with cotton balls. And her squirrels and baby birds LIVE. (Did I mention that I'm afraid of squirrels?)

Courtney's mother is a pediatric oncologist which means she treats kids with cancer. She also has two big brothers, so they're as tough as nails in that

2

house. Her dad works at an advertising agency doing I don't know what. Courtney says he really always wanted to be a rock star. He doesn't look like he could ever be a rock star. He looks like a guy losing his hair who is kind of worried a lot.

So starting in kindergarten Courtney took me in like one of her stray cats. Did I mention she feeds six cats every day in the alley behind her house? The Bilsessers have two dogs, and three parakeets that live inside. The reason Courtney and I are best friends and closer than sisters is simple. When I tell her stuff like the Aspen trees have eyes in their bark and are staring at me, she thinks I'm being funny. She doesn't believe I really mean it. She just smiles and gives me a little shove. I'm literally trying to keep from jumping out of my own skin and she's giggling. You gotta love her for that. I do.

So Courtney Bilsesser is kind of my anchor to anything that's normal. I live with my Grandma whose name is Reneta Bertha Beckdell. My name is Sasha Beckdell Lewis. I'm glad I got Beckdell, and not the Reneta or the Bertha part. Sasha is crazy enough. I call my grandma "Nammy." I guess it's because when I was little I couldn't grit my teeth or something. Sometimes I call her "mom" but I think she likes the "Nammy" thing. We both know she's really my mom without me saying it. My real father was kind of a 'no-show' from the 'get-go' as Nammy says. And my real Mom was never a good driver even though the accident was technically not her fault. So that's left me with Nammy. There are worse places to be left, believe me. And I know.

So it's me and the lady who loves the weather channel, anything with butterscotch, and crossword puzzles.

Courtney says that Nammy is like a cat that was declawed. She doesn't feel comfortable going outdoors because she doesn't have any defenses. Little does she know I'm worse than the declawed cat. I only go out because the law says kids have to go to middle school. If they didn't I'd be parked in front of the TV with Nammy. We'd pick sunflower seed shells out of our teeth and drink diet soda.

TWO

My first real fight with Courtney was about the swim team. I mean real drag down yelling at each other and crying kind of fight. Obviously Courtney can swim. And obviously she's really, really good. She wanted me to join her group of strong, v-back shaped Amazons. They freeze their butts off at all hours and all they get is green hair.

So one day Courtney says she's going out for the swim team. I immediately think about the potential health risks. Getting up before the sun comes up to swim in a freezing cold pool filled with smelly chemicals that I know for a fact cause cancer can't be good for you. Then she says she wants us BOTH to do it. That's when the fighting started. And it lasted for two weeks. For fourteen straight days we didn't say one word to each other.

The weekends weren't as bad as the school

days. I usually always spent every weekend with Courtney but I still had Nammy. I could deal with the weather channel and help her with crossword puzzles.

But the weekdays were a real challenge because we always, always, always eat lunch together. During the fourteen days of silence I just didn't eat at school. Never in a million years would I go into that cafeteria by myself. There is no scarier place in the world than sitting alone in a middle school cafeteria. Remember, I'm an expert on scary things.

Of course Courtney had the whole school who wanted to sit by her. Everyone was thrilled that she didn't have 'the Weirdo' at her sleeve. I know what they call me. I may be a big loser but I'm not totally out of it.

During what I think of as the "ice age," we never once made eye contact. Swim season started. Of course, Courtney didn't just make the team, she was elected captain. She even got to pick out their new swimsuits from a catalog. For the first time, the school had a chance to be good in a girls' sport. All the swimmers got sweatshirts that said, "Pain goes away. Pride stays forever." The first time I saw Courtney in the thing I knew she'd been brainwashed. If there was one thing I knew in my thirteen and a half years on the planet, it was that pain stays forever. Any pain that's real anyway. Pride comes and goes depending on your mood and the people around you and what day of the week it is. It figures that some jock would get it all wrong.

During those two weeks I got to know the janitor, which was a real eye-opener. His name is Jose Hernandez and he used to live in El Salvador. He was studying to be a doctor, but he wanted more for his family so he moved here. Now he has to pick up empty chip bags and soda cans for ten hours a day.

But he's really got a good attitude about it. Before, I never even thought about what pigs most middle school kids are. You'd think they would actually use the trash cans. But I've got a news flash: they don't. And I now completely understand why you can't chew gum in Singapore or wherever it is they've made it against the law. Jose's biggest battle is against chewing gum. He's got a cleaner he made up himself and could probably patent. He mixes paint thinner with Windex and peanut butter. It forms this brown paste which smells like a chemical sandwich. Jose even gave me my own little can of his peanut butter cleaning paste.

I was getting used to the hunger pains of midday and hanging out with Jose. Then, on day fourteen, at four minutes after one o'clock, Courtney walked up to me. She said, "I don't care about you not going out for the swim team anymore."

I didn't think I heard her right and didn't even answer. She continued, "I'll never bring it up again as long as you promise that one time, just once, somewhere in the future, you'll go out for a sports team with me."

I stared at her for awhile savoring my victory. She must have missed me. Either that or she felt sorry for me. I was getting even thinner now that I only ate two meals a day. And both Jose and Nammy said I looked more pale than usual. Looking back, I probably seemed like a baby squirrel or a fallen bird. It was obvious she had to pick me up.

I opened my mouth and was surprised to hear myself say simply and directly, "Okay."

We turned and silently walked to homeroom together. The ice age was over. And I didn't yet realize the enormity of the promise I made. That's the thing about promises. They're easy to make. Keeping them is another story.

THREE

Everybody has an Ashley Aiken. Ashley is one of those people that makes everyone's life a little worse. And I mean everyone. I know Ashley's parents and I swear even they look nervous around her.

Ashley's voice sounds like the brakes on my bike when I go down a steep hill. It's squeaky and shrill and annoying. She has her parents waiting for every command as if they worked for her. I don't really make commands since mostly I'm the person bringing Nammy things. I'm not complaining, because as long as the dirty dishes are loaded into the machine and her soda still has bubbles, Nammy's in her green chair minding her own business.

The good news about Ashley is she doesn't go to school with me. She's better than that. Courtney and I go to Eleanor Roosevelt Middle School. Ashley's parents got special permission for her to go across town to Franklin Middle School. Franklin was built only ten years ago. All the classrooms are big and have bright-colored furniture made out of curvy plastic. Roosevelt's been around forever. Every room smells of layers and layers of old paint and floor wax. All our desks are made of wood and have stuff carved in the top and wobbly legs because everything's been repaired a million times.

So fortunately, I only see Ashley when I pass by her huge house at the end of my block. Nammy and I live in the smallest house on the street, which is just fine. It's only the two of us and I'm afraid of large structures anyway. Plus Nammy's lived here forever.

We just barely squeak by on the social security checks we both get. I get one for not having a Mom anymore, and Nammy gets one for not having a husband anymore. If I could just black out the Home Shopping Channel everything would ease up for us. Nammy sees things for sale and even though it's stuff we don't need, and stuff that we probably don't even really want, she just can't help herself. That's why we have three automatic cat box cleaners (but no cat), all kinds of electric can openers and food slicers, and enough fake jewelry to start our own boutique.

Nammy says it's important to have good costume jewelry in the house. This is in case we're robbed at gunpoint and they want our valuables. The plan is to hand over the fake stuff instead of the real stuff. The only flaw in Nammy's thinking is we don't have any real stuff. If you took a look around our place I don't think you'd find this shocking. But Nammy won't hear a word of my logic. Besides, when she starts talking about gunpoint and robbers I'm up for any plan.

At night, when I'm lying in bed worrying about things like robbers with pistols or a possible invasion of flying grasshoppers, only one thing helps me calm down. I know that any robber with half a brain would go to Ashley Aiken's. They have two brand new Sport Utility Vehicles in their driveway. Every electronic device for sale in the Sharper Image catalog is sitting in their living room. That's the flip side of being a show-off. You make yourself a target.

When I was smaller Ashley thought it was fun to chase me home. If she saw me coming, she'd bound out of her house and come at me. Sometimes she'd hurl rotten apples from the Wallerstein's yard right at my head. I tried all kinds of tactics to get her to stop. I even wrote her a mean note which I claimed was from the police. I put it in her mailbox with a stamp and everything but nothing worked.

Finally I just started walking home the long way, going an extra two blocks north. It meant passing the scariest dog in the world (it doesn't matter that he's behind a fence because he would rip my legs right off if he ever got the chance). But that didn't mean Ashley was out of my life forever. It just meant I didn't have to worry about the apple assault for a while.

FOUR

Eighth grade was supposed to be hard but so far it didn't seem that way. They made a lot of noise about preparing us for the future, which means high school. But really, the year is only different because we have to do the science fair. They talk about it like one of us is going to clone a sheep or something. I bet not one kid in my whole grade will get a job in science. We've probably got a whole mess of kids who will end up in food services. I don't see any kind of cooking fair being planned.

Courtney has no science fair anxiety because her mother is a doctor. Plus Courtney's whole idea of fun is growing things and watching the progress. My idea of a good time is killing germs. I read about that flesh-eating virus and the recent outbreak of tuberculosis. For awhile there I was washing my hands about forty times a day. Then I read that people who do that are crazy. Then I started to go crazy just thinking about how crazy I was being and I had to make myself stop. I still put a paper towel over the doorknob when I leave the bathroom, but I don't think anyone's going to lock me up for that.

Courtney and I both have Ms. Biculos as our science teacher. Ms. Biculos wears high heels and dark suits that make her look like a flight attendant. I figure it's because she's only in her second year of teaching. She hasn't figured out yet that she should be in track shoes and ugly pants. Ms. Biculos came to us all the way from Florida. She used to work in a real lab doing stuff for the space program. Shelly Wetterling said she got fired when a new satellite blew up, which cost like a billion dollars. Shelly said she was one of the only girl scientists, so it figures they'd blame her. I'm really curious what Ms. Biculos did to make it explode. I want to ask her all the time but I don't want to embarrass her. I'm just hoping we'll be alone one day and she'll be in a confessing mood.

The first Friday in October they made us turn in our science fair proposals. Courtney is growing brine shrimp in water with different levels of salt. I would never, ever, in a million, trillion years do this. I can't stand the smell of fish and I'm afraid of shrimp (Don't they look like they could bite? And what's the story with those tails?). Plus everyone knows that water projects are twice as much work as land ones.

The first proposal I submitted for the fair was rejected. I wanted to work with an exterminator. The school hires this guy to spray bug killer in back of the cafeteria. He drives a pick-up truck with a dented metal spider on the door. He usually wears a blue plastic suit with yellow kitchen gloves. Nobody believes me, but I know for a fact that he wears swim goggles when he's spraying. We could have worked together on a nice project involving toxic chemicals, but they wouldn't hear of it.

My second proposal got me in trouble. I wanted to use surveillance to determine how teachers spent their time outside of class. Were they in the teacher's lounge? The bathroom? The back parking lot sneaking cigarettes? Did any of them spend time together? Could you make any connection to what they did while not teaching with how happy they seemed in the classroom? I wanted to put these collars on their ankles that were designed to keep track of hunting dogs. I saw them for sale in the back of a magazine at the dentist's office. It was a big project, but that's not what they had a problem with.

Ms. Biculos got all pink in the face when she read my proposal paragraph. She asked me if I'd shown my proposal to anyone. I don't think she believed me when I said no. She made me go see Mr. Hockstatter who is the principal. He then got all pink in the face and said he'd never had a cigarette in the back parking lot. That was so weird, because who ever said he did?

After that, they assigned me to grow mold on bread in different light conditions. Just the idea of it makes me want to throw up. We've been growing mold in different light conditions in our kitchen for as long as I can remember. I haven't learned one thing from it and obviously neither has Nammy.

FIVE

After swim season, girls had basketball or gymnastics to pick from. I can't do a cartwheel or a handstand so gymnastics was out. This left basketball, which requires all kinds of skills. You can't just learn them in one day even if you wanted to. And I didn't want to.

Courtney doesn't even try at basketball and of course she's the best in our grade. She's goofed around with her brothers since she was a toddler and that had been enough. Now she can shoot from anywhere and the ball just goes in. She always looks sort of surprised as if it was some kind of accident. She can jump better than all of the girls and most of the boys. She's sort of a natural player. So when Courtney asked me to try out, I had the good sense to play along with her. Once everyone saw me play, any fool would see I wouldn't be helping the team.

Coach Moshofsky, the girl's basketball coach, really loves winning so I knew my plan was good. You should have seen her face when I walked into the gym. She looked like she'd bit into a sour tangerine as she stared at my thin legs. She then realized that I was there to compete. I could tell right away that the idea frightened her.

Over the next three afternoons I jammed my right finger so bad it had to be put in a splint, cracked the glass in one of the high gymnasium windows (bad pass), missed every shot I took, and accidentally tripped fellow teammate Jessica Pendergast, causing her to miss the entire season with torn knee cartilage. There seemed to be no limit to the damage I would cause if I continued.

But Coach Moshofsky didn't want to do anything that would upset Courtney. She needed to make sure I would walk away with my head held high. So instead of just cutting me, she called me into her office. Courtney was breathless, "Coach wants to see you. Sasha, I think you have a shot."

Part of my strategy was to act like I really cared. I tried to look as sincere as possible. "I've got my fingers crossed," I said to her.

Coach Moshofsky's office was small and filled with dusty junk from years of sporting events. I noticed a bunch of stuffed hogs, each of them holding a blue basketball. The office smelled like wet socks and vitamins with iron.

"Have a seat, Sasha."

I sat down in the one available chair and looked straight at the linoleum floor.

"You put a lot of effort into your basketball try-out."

I nodded.

"In the past, I've never seen you put in much effort in PE class."

I shrugged.

"I think the other girls were impressed."

I'd made an impression. That was for sure. "If I can't find room for you, I don't want you to feel bad."

I tried to make sure there was zero joy in my voice:

"I'm not going to make the team?"

Coach cleared her throat, "I don't think so."

I looked up and was surprised to see that she actually felt sorry for me. I seized the opportunity.

My lower lip trembled as I spoke. "If I can't be on the team I don't think I'll be able to play basketball in regular PE class. It would be too painful."

And so Coach Moshofsky and I cut a deal. In order to protect my fragile mental health, I was excused from PE—for the rest of the term.

This gave me a free period every day to catch up with Jose the Janitor. Jose had enrolled in night school and was studying to be a nurse. If he couldn't be a doctor he wanted to at least get back in medicine. I started testing him on the stuff he learned the night before. That's why I now know the difference between a feeding cup and a feeding beaker. And, I can answer the all-important question: "How many fluid ounces will the standard male bedside incontinent device hold?"

So for nine solid weeks I ate Milk Duds, went on-line, and studied the nursing catalog. I'd never had it this good. And Courtney was okay with it because I'd tried to play a sport.

At the end of the term, when I saw the "PASS" in the space next to Physical Education, I was very proud. For a brief moment I thought maybe they were right. Pain goes away. Pride stays forever.

SIX

The Bilsesser's was the only other place where I would ever spend the night. Even though they had two dogs the size of pack mules, and a cage with parakeets that obviously wanted to peck my eyes out if they were given a chance, I was able to calm down enough to sleep for at least part of the night. It helped that Courtney's mother was a real doctor. If one of the dogs bit me at least they wouldn't have to call 911.

She and Nammy had nothing in common. I don't remember Dr. Bilsesser once sitting with her feet up. I've also never seen her do a crossword puzzle or suck on a butterscotch drop. She's always moving. And even when she's asking us questions, half the time she answers them herself. Then she jumps to the next topic before you can even get going on the first one. If Nammy asks something she waits for the answer. She always wants to know what I think and listens even when I'm just making stuff up (which is about half the time). I could get a bat and go downtown and hit a bunch of people in the mall and come home and tell Nammy. She'd listen to my story and then tell me they deserved it. You get the picture. She keeps the curtains closed twenty four seven. I'm kind of the light around the place.

Which isn't to say Dr. and Mr. Bilsesser don't think Courtney's great. But they've got Wally and Ned and jobs that they're still thinking about when they come home. They exercise every day and are always rushing to a yoga class or the running club. They eat fresh food, not stuff that's been in cans or frozen. They go to the market every two seconds. Plus they attend neighborhood meetings and parties where people use little napkins and eat stuff on toothpicks. Nammy doesn't do any of that so she's got lots of time.

As a rule I don't eat anything stuck on a toothpick. When I was in the second grade I sucked too hard on a fudgesicle stick after trying to get the very last part of the chocolate taste off. It broke in two and one of the pieces went straight back and got stuck in my throat. I had to go to the hospital. I've never seen Nammy so upset. She was crying and swearing all at the same time. She never drives because of what happened to Mom, but she tried to and the car wouldn't start, so Mr. Wallerstein from down the street took us.

By the time Nammy had filled out the hospital forms and they finally got the doctor in the room I'd swallowed the piece of stuck wood. I didn't even know it. All that was left was a big scratch in the back of my throat. So instead of giving me any medicine they gave Nammy some to calm herself down. She got so tired from everything that she fell asleep in the taxi going home. Me and the driver (who was really nice) had to drag her inside. We just couldn't wake her up. Afterwards the taxi guy stayed for a cup of hot chocolate and wouldn't take any money which was so nice I couldn't believe it. Nammy said it gave her faith in the system which I guess meant the system of taxi drivers.

After all that we never had any kind of ice cream in the house anymore. Nammy said we just didn't need the aggravation. I'm okay with that because ice cream isn't as good as chocolate in my book. Or custard. Or most kinds of pies.

SEVEN

It was February and I was sleeping over on a Saturday night. Courtney stopped channel surfing and made us watch a soccer game on the Spanish-language channel. She said how big the stadium was and what cool orange shirts they were wearing. I should have figured out something was up.

The second thing that happened was that Courtney started acting crazy after school. We'd be walking home, talking about Duncan Frye's irritating laugh or Mary Tignanello's new braces. Then suddenly she'd see something out of the corner of her eye and shriek. Since she'd never been afraid of anything before, ever, this was big news. So if she was scared, I was out of my mind. And so we'd end up running. And she didn't stop right away. She ran for blocks. But I didn't think twice when she said she'd seen a huge spider. Maybe she'd finally gotten some common sense.

Then she saw hairy men in the shadows. Birds with big claws. A bat on a telephone pole. Pretty soon we were running at least half of the way home every day. In the beginning I was out of breath and bright red for two hours afterwards. But after a few weeks of the constant mad dashes I hardly noticed the difference. It had always taken us forty-five minutes to get to her house. Now we were in the front door in less than twenty. We now had extra time before our favorite soap opera started.

Courtney took to kicking an old volleyball against the wall of her garage. I had no interest, so I sat in the grass and watched. But sometimes the ball would go off all crazy and end up next to me. When this happened Courtney would yell for me to kick it back.

And I still didn't put two and two together. I ran and kicked a ball and didn't realize that she had me in training. But that wasn't all. She suddenly became this insane hockey fan. She talked about hockey all the time and even had a favorite team. She'd draw these diagrams on notebook paper and talk about the forwards and the goalie and how they passed to each other and moved the puck around and what it meant to be "off-sides." I was bored out of my mind. I figured she'd get over it like a new tee shirt or something. Now I can't believe the planning that went into the whole scheme.

Her brother Wally started kicking that old volleyball for about fifteen minutes, too. When his kicks went bad I had to go twice as far to get them. Wally started giving me advice when I booted the stupid thing back. He'd yell all kinds of stuff about 'follow through.' Then the other brother, Ned, got in on the action. When Ned started telling me stuff I got scared. His upper lip lately had this layer of brown hair. It wasn't a real moustache, but it wasn't not a moustache either. And I'm afraid of people with moustaches. Plus Ned is the oldest boy I've ever really talked to. He's got friends who can drive cars so he gets dropped off after school like he's a grown-up. He's always got a bag of cold French fries from some drive-thru place they stopped at on the way home.

At first Ned just stood in the driveway and watched. But then he started telling me to drop my head a little when I kicked the ball and to put more guts in my foot. I didn't have any idea what he was talking about. The whole thing was just crazy.

Then one day it happened. Courtney couldn't even bring herself to look at me when she did it. She says oh-so-casually, "Spring sports are coming up. I thought we'd go out for soccer."

I swallowed hard. Soccer was a sport for girls who had thick legs and strong bodies. They weren't afraid of balls whizzing around like cannon projectiles. People kicked at other people on purpose and slammed their heads into leather. They also slammed into each other. You wore cleats which were so scary, and molded plastic pieces strapped to your shins. Soccer players ran around on fields like packs of wild animals scrambling after what in ancient times had been the inflated stomach of a goat. It was barbaric.

All I said back was, "Soccer?"

Courtney still wasn't even looking at me.

"Yeah. It's super fun. And I think you'll be real good at it."

My idea of super fun is a field trip to a security systems company. And the list of things I'm real good at could fit on a postage stamp. I stopped dead in my tracks.

"Really?"

She had to meet my gaze. And when she did she looked guilty.

"You'll try out—right?"

That night I thought about it. I was looking through the newspaper and cutting out all the articles about accidents (I glue them into a huge scrapbook I've kept for the last five years). I figured soccer try-outs could end up being a good thing. I'd never played the game so there was no way I would make the team. With any luck I could weasel out of gym class again. The secret would be to really try. Sports types were real suckers for sweaty effort.

I finished pasting the article about the car crash at the railroad crossing next to the story about the man who got his shirt stuck in the printing press and lost two fingers. Then the doorbell rang. Nammy told me not to answer it, which was our policy, especially if it was dark outside. Now that her hearing wasn't so good, she rarely spoke anymore. Instead, she yelled all of her instructions. Her voice was loud enough to be heard down the street. It was followed by Courtney's voice coming through the front door. "It's me! It's just Courtney!"

So of course I answered it. Courtney was standing on the doormat with a bag in her hand. Her face was flushed from the cold night air. I could see Mr. Bilsesser seated behind the wheel of his car at the curb.

"Here. We got you these. They were on sale so it's no big deal."

Before I could respond she pushed a heavy plastic bag into my arms. She turned with a wave and in a few effortless strides was in her car. I shut the door because Nammy was still yelling: "Don't answer the door!"

I went straight to my room and sat down on the bed.

Inside the plastic bag was a cardboard box containing a pair of shoes. They were black leather and had three white stripes along the sides. I flipped them over and stared at the hard white plastic soles. They were studded with raised round bumps like an oversized kid's Lego. I held them in my hands as if they were artifacts from an historic dig. They may as well have been. Nammy and I didn't own anything athletic. Not unless you count her fourth husband Rayford's old bowling ball in the hall closet.

I held the shoes right up to my nose and inhaled big. They smelled like cattle. Or at least what I imagine cattle smell like. They had a strong, outdoor, somewhat masculine odor. I couldn't help myself. As much as I hated the idea of soccer, I wanted to try them on.

I was surprised that they made me seem a lot taller. It must be because of the cleats. I clattered around my room for awhile certain I'd get a blister or strain something. But they fit perfectly. Finally, after an hour, I picked up the telephone and called Courtney. She answered on the first ring.

"Bilsesser residence."

I skipped right to what she wanted to hear.

"I'm wearing the shoes."

Her joyful shriek was numbing.

EIGHT

Most of the stuff I own comes from garage sales or second-hand stores. We've been going to the Salvation Army and Goodwill our whole lives. At least I have anyway. Nammy's right that you can get good stuff for cheap at these places. But that doesn't mean I want the entire world to know we shop 'used.' So I got all worked up when Ashley Aiken saw us head into the Salvation Army. It's one thing to go there because you *want* to. It's another to shop there because you *have* to.

Ashley was waiting impatiently in her mother's brand new car at the time. As soon as she saw me she started to laugh. No matter who you are, or what you're doing, when someone laughs at you and you haven't told a joke or made a face or goofed on yourself, it makes you feel rotten. You just can't help but wonder if you didn't zip up your pants or something. Ashley laughed and she laughed hard. Then she pretended to throw an apple at my head and mouthed "See ya around!"

My face was all red as we came through the thrift store's front door. Mrs. Aiken was standing at the counter arguing with the woman at the register. She was arguing about some tax deduction while holding up the entire line. It wasn't long before the front door of the store flew open and Ashley appeared. She didn't step one foot into the room, shouting instead from her spot: "What is taking so long?!"

Mrs. Aiken's head snapped around. It was clear who called the shots. Mrs. Aiken gave up her argument with the woman and headed toward Ashley. "I'm coming, dear," she spoke in an unnatural voice.

Ashley shot me a parting look that said 'loser' and headed back to their car. It was only then that I heard the sound. A clattering, clicking sound. I moved to the front window to get a better view.

On Ashley's feet were soccer shoes.

NINE

I think what happened the next day was totally Ashley Aiken's fault. On the ride home I was real quiet and Nammy figured out something was wrong.

"Are you sick or something?" Nammy asked me.

I couldn't tell her how I never wanted to go in the Salvation Army again. I might end up owning some old shirt of Ashley Aiken's! I'd rather die. So I just slouched deeper into the bus seat and shrugged. "Have we ever *given* anything to the Salvation Army?" I asked. "Or do we only buy stuff there?"

Nammy snorted through her nose. "Of course we give them things. All the time."

I didn't say that I never once remembered us donating anything. I didn't mention the fact that you couldn't close any of our closets or drawers either.

Nammy must have thought about my comment, though. The next morning she loaded two large garbage bags of stuff onto my red wagon. I offered to help, but she said she'd rather walk by herself. She never left the house two days in a row so I knew she was making some kind of statement.

The store has a swinging door on the roof for making charity donations. According to Nammy, she placed her purse next to the trash bags in the wagon. She must have been distracted when she dumped the stuff in. She ended up donating her purse to the Salvation Army.

A more regular person might have just called the Salvation Army. But it was Sunday, and Nammy figured no one would answer the phone. So she decided to take matters into her own hands. She'd go in after the purse.

She positioned my old red wagon right underneath the swinging roof door and climbed up. Somehow she got herself through the swinging door into the drop-off box. She was lucky it was filled with old clothes because she sort of tumbled in. She eventually found her purse and tried to get back through.

What Nammy didn't know was that lately, homeless people had been stealing from the drop-off boxes. I don't really understand how a homeless person can be stealing. The Salvation Army's goal is to help the people who are homeless. So anyway, the police now drove by a few times a day. That's why they were there when Nammy's head popped out of the donation box.

I was home when the police called and said they had my Nammy in custody. I have an uncle, but he's really only a half-uncle because he and my Mom had different fathers. He lives in Boston and calls Nammy every Christmas. Otherwise, we don't hear from him. Nammy says he was always more trouble than he was worth but I think that was because his father was the one Nammy liked the best. His father left her one day a long, long time ago. He went out to play golf and he just never came back.

I've only seen Uncle Arnold twice in my life and I don't remember either time. I guess he's real smart because he works in a lab with genes. Up until about a year ago I thought that meant he made pants. We hadn't studied genes yet in science and no one ever explains anything around here. You just get it from hanging around and figuring it out yourself. I think Uncle Arnold might come over more if I weren't in the picture. My guess is that he doesn't want to end up raising me so he stays away.

I thought about trying to find his number because this seemed like a family emergency. But then I realized even if I could find the number, what could he do? He was on the other side of the country and I was here in Oregon.

I put on my jacket with the big hood. I didn't want anyone to see me going into the police station. And I silently cursed the Aikens for all the trouble they caused.

TEN

I ran all the way to the police station. By the time I got there, I was breathing funny and seeing spots. I was worried sick, imagining Nammy in all kinds of trouble. Instead I found her drinking hot cider with her new friends, Officers Crowley and Morales. She was even giving suggestions on junk-food preparation to the office manager. She looked disappointed, not relieved, when I walked in, and didn't even try to hide it from me.

It turned out that once the officers heard about Nammy's five husbands and her streak of incredibly bad luck (which probably included a few words about me ending up on her doorstep), they were all ears. No one seemed to care anymore about the Salvation Army box. They weren't going to press any charges—she was now their new mascot.

I stood around like a party pooper as Nammy gathered up her things. Once we had left the station though, it was a different story. Nammy started moaning about all the injuries she got in the fall inside the box. Her back was killing her and her hip felt funny. She even said her vision was all messed up. By the time we got home I felt like an old lady myself.

Nammy said she had to rest and went straight to her room. I went to the kitchen because I hadn't eaten anything yet all day. I poured myself a bowl of cereal even though we didn't have any milk. I spread peanut butter inside some celery sticks, which is what I practically live on. I took my food into the bathroom and started a hot tub. I add dishwashing liquid because that makes a lot of good bubbles. I do this when I want to feel that everything is okay in the world. Plus I'm cold a lot and it's the fastest way to heat myself up.

I don't know why but I got in with all my clothes on. They separated away from me and floated, swishing up against my skin like wet leaves. I wondered where the boy I would grow up to marry was right at this very moment. Was he taking a bath too? Maybe eating cereal without milk or celery with peanut butter? I wondered if we already had a connection and didn't know it. Maybe later on we could link up the dots which would form some kind of line that would lead us back to some place where it was possible we were thinking the same thing at the same time. That's what happens I guess, when you spend a lot of time alone. Or when you live with someone who's sixty-five years older than you are. You do a lot of dreaming.

ELEVEN

I wrapped my new soccer shoes in old Christmas tissue and took them to school Monday morning. Courtney was jumpy and excited all day, which is just not like her. She'd put a lot of effort into her plan and was feeling pretty good about it. I found out that many girls had played soccer since 'K-league,' which meant kindergarten I guess. So they'd been on a soccer field for eight years. This was music to my ears. I'd never make the team.

After our last class Courtney and I went to the gym to change. I felt like a spy because I wasn't there for the same reason as the other girls. Hiding my true feelings made me feel dangerous, like a risk-taker. This was about as far from the real me as you can get.

It turned out that Coach Moshofsky didn't coach soccer. Instead, the school hired someone different. Someone entirely different.

There wasn't anybody in our school like Otto. There wasn't anybody I'd ever seen in real life like him either. Otto Czernin looked like he belonged on TV. Maybe selling toothpaste with special whiteners or a fancy sports car. He was twenty-three and tall, with brown curly hair and yesterday's beard growth. His gray eyes swirled around, making him look like a wild dog or a circus performer. His body was one hundred percent muscle and his legs looked scary strong. They scared me anyway.

Otto had played for the Hungarian Olympic team and then hurt himself. After the injury, his soccer career was over. He came to America to study sports medicine but that didn't work out either. So now he was getting a degree in electrical engineering at the local university. He planned on going back to Eastern Europe to make their lights brighter or something.

But Otto loved soccer and he missed it. It was worth it to him to help some American girls learn something about the most beautiful sport in the world.

The second Courtney saw him on the field, she changed. She was cheerfully talking about the tryouts when she suddenly stopped mid-sentence. Her eyes were riveted on Otto.

Now I've known Courtney liking a boy for a week or maybe even a month. But it's never any big deal and she doesn't even talk about it really. That is until Otto came into the picture. He had more appeal for us than we ever knew the opposite sex could possess. He was, in short, the coolest guy we'd ever met. It took the rest of us all of thirty seconds to figure it out. It took Courtney one glance.

After Otto introduced himself he asked us all to run four laps around the field. Courtney had said she'd be right next to me and we'd go at my pace. That was now ancient history. Courtney took off in a sprint, running as fast as she could. Chelsea Luzzato, who was considered the best runner in our class, couldn't catch her. I just stayed in the middle of the pack.

Otto rewarded Courtney with a small smile. He didn't say anything to her, but his smile was enough. She took her hair out of her ponytail and let it loose (which she never did) and waited patiently for his next instruction. I was shocked.

We next had to dribble a ball through a long course of orange cones. Courtney didn't even check to see what line I was in. She effortlessly worked her way around the obstacles at high speed. She was going to make it absolutely clear who the best girl soccer player was.

I'd never seen her try so hard at anything. It was like watching a tornado take shape.

TWELVE

Before, my plan had been to just make it look like I cared. Now I was really, truly trying. But it didn't matter because even giving it my full effort I was horrible. Thanks to Courtney's daily sprints home I was now at least an average runner. But during the cone course it was obvious I had zero control of the ball.

On my first touch I sent it flying way too far. When I went to get the ball, I tripped and fell. On my second attempt I went so slowly I heard some of the girls snicker. I don't even blame them because I was really holding things up. The final trial of the day was drop kicks. Because of Courtney, I could at least boot the thing part way across the field. Courtney of course had the hardest kick by far. She sent the ball from midfield all the way to the goal line. She apologized after her turn for not really getting her foot underneath it right.

We ended with stretching exercises, which Otto

asked Courtney to lead. This was about the only thing I was good at. Because I don't have any muscles I can pretty much bend in any direction. It's kind of like watching a flexible stick insect. I can really fold over.

Otto clapped his hands, thanked us all for coming and said he'd see us tomorrow. He added that he thought we had a lot of talent. He was looking at Courtney and I could see her cheeks burn red.

We all walked back to the gym in silence. That's what real greatness will do. It shuts you up.

Once in the confines of the girls' locker room, we all just sort of exploded. Helen Herlihy started giggling and couldn't stop. Katie Lopez instantly got the hiccups and Rosie Chung started singing. Christine Blum jumped on the benches and did this gross dance she saw on MTV. Amy Maclellan took off most of her clothes and put them on her head. And Lauren Fenulli opened a huge bag of Doritos and everyone began stuffing their faces, talking as they chewed. It was totally crazy.

Suddenly, it didn't matter to anyone that I was Courtney's loser friend. I'd been there. I'd witnessed the miracle. I was part of the group.

I was surprised at how good that felt.

When Courtney and I walked home, she talked about him the whole way. I meant it when I told her I hoped I made the team. But Otto had to cut seven players and I was clearly one of the worst girls.

Courtney stopped looking off into the distance and focused on me. It was as if everything else I'd said in the last hour was just noise. This she heard. When she spoke it was in a whisper: "No. I want you to be there. I want you to be part of this."

I could tell she really meant it. I nodded back. I knew that she still cared about me, even with Otto now in the picture.

When I got into the house Nammy was asleep in her chair. That was good because I thought she might be worried since I was so late. After I had some celery with peanut butter, I took out my soccer shoes. The bottoms were now coated with mud and grass. I put them outside because there are millions of bacteria and germs in fresh dirt. But later I couldn't sleep because I was worried about them. I know, who would go into our backyard to steal a pair of soccer shoes? But I still got up and brought them back in. I cleaned off the dirt with a steak knife and wrapped them in a bag. When I fell asleep it was a thick kind of sleep. It's like where someone's frozen you solid and when you wake up you don't even know where you are because it's so different from what was going on in your sleeping head. That's how far away I was.

And then I remembered where I'd been in my dream. I was on a big green field running in the full sun. And I was kicking a soccer ball.

THIRTEEN

For the next two days we continued to practice. I realized I could break down the girls into four groups. The first was the Stars. This was Courtney and her smaller Stars, Drina Archer and Helen Herlihy. The Stars were always at the right place at the right time. Their bodies moved in ways that made you stand up and take notice. They had some inner feeling about the game that the rest of us didn't have. They were the bright spots in the field.

Behind the Stars were the Strong Players. They were good athletes, played other sports and probably walked early as babies. After the Strong Players were the Players, and this group was the largest. These girls at least knew what they were doing and were pretty good at sports. They probably all had Dads who watched ESPN with them or something. The Players had good days and bad days and things they could do and things they couldn't, but they always knew what was going on. After the Players there was a group of Losers.

I think it's important to say that I was not the loser of the Losers. I would have been if I hadn't been running and kicking with Courtney beforehand. The Losers had all kinds of reasons for being there. Two girls each had a big sister who was a good soccer player. They didn't have any talent or interest in soccer, but were just expected to play. Three of the loser girls had just shown up looking for something to do. They were open-faced, and without worry or fear. They were no good at soccer but it didn't seem to matter. They were up for some fun, and didn't really care if it didn't work out.

That wasn't the attitude of the last four Losers. They were strugglers. They tried and tried hard, but their bodies didn't cooperate. When they kicked the ball they often missed and got the air. When they ran their legs would twist up, or cramp, or wear out. They got side aches and shin splints and headaches. They were always thirsty and tired and sweaty.

I at least knew I was a Loser, which wasn't true of all of us. Occasionally, a Loser thinks they are really a Player, or even worse, a Strong Player. Anyone who is jumping two whole categories is really out of touch with the world. This is a Super Loser. Your heart has to go out to them, but it doesn't. Instead you just want to scream at them. You want to tell them they should have signs on their backs saying, "Cut Me. I deserve it."

Otto pretended he couldn't figure this out in ten minutes when I know he did. Instead he shouted encouraging things like "go to the ball" and "put your body into it." Like the rest of the girls, I was watching him.

He only got better. He came out to demonstrate how to kick and asked us to get in close. That was like throwing out bread for a pack of seagulls by the dump. We were right next to him in a flash. He had to tell us to step back because he probably couldn't even breathe.

On the third day Otto came out on the field and played with us. He picked out Courtney to be on his team, and she never looked so happy. Courtney and Otto ran down the field passing back and forth, while we stood with our mouths open. Otto could do anything with a soccer ball. Just watching his feet made me dizzy.

When I wasn't at practice I couldn't help but think about him. It was like I had a can of soda open inside my stomach and it was him and it was just constantly releasing these "Otto bubbles." They would float right up through my body and then pop at the top of my head with a fizzle. It left me feeling achy and kind of confused and made it harder to breathe and eat my celery sticks with peanut butter.

At the end of tryouts he gave a speech thanking us for our efforts. He said he was sorry that we couldn't have a team with twenty-seven girls. He really looked sad about it.

A list would be posted in the morning on the door of the gym. We walked off the field knowing that we'd just had three of the most important days of our lives.

All of us walked off the field except Courtney. She waited until the last girl was a good twenty yards away. Then I saw her go to Otto and say something that no one could hear. I saw his face; he was surprised. He said something back and she shook her head. She then abruptly turned and started off in a jog after the rest of us.

But I kept my eyes on Otto, who was now staring at me.

FOURTEEN

Courtney used a pay phone to call her father to pick her up. I think it was because she didn't feel like talking. In the locker room, I couldn't ask her why she said something to Otto. She didn't volunteer anything either. She was just real quiet and looked sort of defeated.

When I got home, Nammy was doing a crossword puzzle. She had a clear plastic bag over her head, with purplish goop on her hair. This meant she was dying it but this didn't always work right. She always missed big spots and ended up looking like a cheetah in the back.

Nammy knew I'd been trying out for soccer but she didn't know anything about sports. She only understood bowling which she'd done a lot when she was younger. Her fourth husband, Rayford, had been in a league. She still had her turquoise colored "Bay

City Bowler" shirt. She didn't fit into it anymore. Nammy says people are just like old dogs. They get thick in the middle, their heads hang lower, and they have eyes that look like someone spilled milk in them.

Nammy called out for me to bring her an appetizer plate. I'd always put pickles, olives and crackers on a tray with a can of sardines. That's where I draw the line. I won't open the sardine tin. Just the smell of those oily little fish makes me sick. I also brought a Diet Coke with a lot of ice. She smiled big when she saw it all.

After my celery and peanut butter I cleaned my soccer shoes. I kept the box they came in, and I wrapped them up in the tissue. I put them all the way in the back of my closet, which is where I keep the big trunk I have of my Mom's stuff. I had promised myself that I wouldn't open the trunk so much. But this time I couldn't help myself. I opened it and got out my Mom's old blue raincoat. I put it on, even though it was way too big for me. I always think I can still smell her when I have on that coat. I'm pretty sure I'm just imagining it because it's been so many years now.

I got out my Mom's yearbook from high school. I'd looked at every page so many times I'd memorized them, but it didn't matter. After about an hour of going through the yearbook I went to get some water. That's when I realized that Nammy still had the plastic goop bag on her head. The food on the appetizer had been devoured, and she'd fallen asleep. She must have had the plastic goop bag on for over three hours. It was all bubbly inside, and I couldn't even see her hair anymore.

I woke her up and helped her into the bathroom. She poured water over her head and all the goop came off. Unfortunately, so did most of her hair. I guess the chemicals cooked it or something. Her hair in the back must be stronger because part of it stayed in. She now had a ring of really weird yellow hair like a clown. She was not happy.

After drying off, she tried on a lot of hats but they all looked bad. So I forced myself to be brave and went up to the attic. The attic, of course, is a home for spiders and other very, very scary things. I found some old Halloween costumes, and I was tempted to take a clown wig. Instead, I took out a wig that had long, straight black hair. I think it was from a really bad 'Sonny and Cher' dress-up set. Nammy put it on and looked about a hundred times weirder, but not in her mind. She liked it.

When I finally went to bed it was really late. I knew I'd be so sick the next day. I feel like I'm going to throw up when I don't get enough sleep. Nammy came into my room in the crazy long wig. She kissed me good night like I was a little kid, which she never does anymore.

She stood in the doorway and sang for awhile: "I got you, babe."

FIFTEEN

The next day I was so exhausted I could barely get going in the morning. I even drank two extra teaspoons of instant coffee but it didn't help. It only made it taste really gross.

When I got to school I was late and went straight to homeroom. Courtney was in her seat smiling which she does a lot. I was going to tell her about Nammy's hair falling out when she blurted out: "Did you go look to see who made the soccer team?"

I thought she was being a show-off, which isn't like her at all.

"Like you ever thought you wouldn't?"

She rolled her eyes.

"You should look at the list."

Maybe there was some kind of joke on it or maybe some surprise about Otto. Whatever it was made her all giggly. I had avoided the list since it was just something to make me feel bad. Now I was rolling my eyes.

"Just tell me."

But she wouldn't. That made me mad. But Courtney kept smiling and didn't seem to mind. Once the bell rang she grabbed my sleeve.

"Come on. We'll go look."

I went along because what else was I supposed to do? Courtney was moving fast now and we bumped into a few people. They all smiled at her like it was no big deal. They glared at me like I'd just given them a bleeding bruise.

When we got to the gym a few girls were standing by the door. They stepped aside because most people just naturally step aside when they see Courtney.

The first thing I saw on the list was my name. I just stared. Courtney was just about to explode at this point.

"Well? What do you think?!"

I couldn't even speak. I looked again because what was my name doing up there?

Courtney put her hand on my shoulder and spun me around. "You made the team! Can you believe it?"

Obviously I couldn't. I looked back at the piece of paper. "It must be wrong."

Courtney couldn't take it anymore. She was insistent now. "You're on the team. You made the cut. We're going to play soccer."

I turned and flew right past her into the girls' bathroom across the hall. I went for the first open stall door and turned the lock on the door.

"Sasha! What's going on?" I heard.

It was Courtney and she sounded upset. I didn't answer. In the hallway the bell rang, echoing in the tiled room. I could hear the other girls leave the bathroom and head to class.

But not Courtney. The next thing I knew, she was in the next stall. She was standing on the toilet seat, peering down at me over the divider.

"What's wrong?"

I looked up at her and when I did my eyes were suddenly all watery. My nose felt tight like the air in it went straight down into my lungs in a weird and maybe even dangerous way. Speaking was going to be a problem. She continued:

"Aren't you happy?"

I nodded my head and was able to murmur: "Yeah."

She looked confused. "Then why are you hiding in the bathroom?"

My ears were burning now, too. It was like someone lit a match inside and the flames were leaping upwards. I managed to say: "Because I'm afraid it will go away."

She answered "What will go away?"

I finally answered, "The feeling. The feeling of being really happy."

Courtney's brow knitted. If she wasn't careful she would have lines in her forehead when she was older. "You're crazy."

I felt pretty sure I wasn't going to cry so I said: "You just now figured that out?"

That made her smile. I think she had a lot invested in my being about a hundred times more normal than I actually am. I continued: "You better get going or you'll be late to math."

That got her. Math was one of her favorite subjects. She jumped down off the toilet seat and ran from the room.

"Congratulations, you nut!" she called over her shoulder.

When I was sure she was gone I put my head in my hands. My ears weren't really on fire and my breathing was returning to normal. Once someone like me starts crying it could go on for days or even weeks. The secret was to just never start no matter what.

Eventually I thought of what it'd be like on the soccer team with Courtney. And with Otto. For the first time all morning I smiled.

SIXTEEN

In science class, Ms. Biculos was taking us into the library. We had to do research for the dreaded science fair. I was supposed to be looking for books about mold and writing facts on index cards. Instead, I only pretended to work. I was really trying to lower my blood pressure and stop freaking out about soccer. Obviously Courtney had cut some kind of deal with Otto. There's no way I deserved to be on the team. What was she thinking?

I immediately started picturing all the ways I could die on a soccer field. If I ran into a goal post the head injury alone would kill me. Or if it didn't, I'd end up in a group home. I'd spend the rest of my days on earth making things out of Popsicle sticks.

After I got tired of worrying about that, I moved on to other possible problems. Being kicked is not my idea of a good time. I know for a fact that shin guards should be made out of metal. And why weren't players forced to wear padding and a helmet? If you're a kid it's against the law to ride your bike without protective headgear. You can't play t-ball when you're tiny unless you wear a big plastic hat. Obviously someone hasn't been paying attention. I decided I would make it my crusade to change the sport. I'd first convince our team, and then all the teams in the league. We should wear thick padded pants, football helmets, as well as elbow and wrist guards. My final, and most brilliant addition, would be the introduction of soft-tipped shoes. They would be designed to lessen the blow a player felt when someone kicked them.

I realized that it might be hard to kick the ball with soft-tipped soccer shoes. But I think safety should always be the first thing athletes and fans think of. For example, if I were in charge of diving, I would get rid of the high board. There is no reason on earth anyone needs to jump, much less dive, off something that far off the ground.

I wrote all my new soccer plans carefully down on my science index cards. After I'd written down my ideas I was feeling sort of normal. I had some time left so I went and got my favorite book which is called "Anomalies of Nature." I am certain that the school has no idea that this book is part of their collection. I discovered it while on a mission to find the oldest book in the library. It turns out there is an older one

on covered wagons but I'd never come upon anything this good. I knew it right away.

"Anomalies of Nature" is really, really old. The
pages have turned color and are crisp and hard on the
edges. But the photographs are what this book is all
about. It's basically a freak show. There are pictures
of Siamese twins, a snake with two heads, and a
woman with a full beard and moustache. And that's
just for starters. There is a cow with five legs, a frog
with part of his brain on the outside, and a man with a
foot the size of a suitcase. The foot is all covered in
spots and scales. You just can't take your eyes off it.

I've always wanted to check the book out and
take it home. But I know if our librarian, Ms. Tartuffe,
saw the pictures she'd take it away for good. So I
have to read it when I can, which is about once a
week. Even though the pictures are the best part, the
stories of the people are great, too. I like the story of
the woman with the beard and the moustache that goes
all the way to the floor. She worked in a circus and
married a man who was an acrobat. They had four
boys and one of them was born with webbed feet.
There isn't a picture of him, which I think is very un-
fair. I'm glad she found someone to marry and he let
her live her own life. He didn't pressure her to shave
off the beard although I don't really know why she
didn't. She would have looked a lot better.

When I search through the book I get sad. Not
because of the strange stuff but because the book is

so old. I know that all the people in the pictures are now dead. It's a weird feeling. Kind of like watching a black and white movie on cable TV. You're enjoying it and then thinking none of the people are even around anymore. It makes you suddenly feel real lonely.

My favorite person in the book is a tiny man named Leon Rildenstein. The picture shows him standing next to a squirrel on its hind legs. Leon isn't very much bigger than the squirrel, and they are both holding nuts.

When I look at the picture I can tell Leon is afraid of the squirrel. I understand. If there were a squirrel my size looking at me with his sharp claws and pointy teeth, I'd be afraid, too.

SEVENTEEN

For the rest of the day I tried not to obsessively think about soccer. But Jose was really happy because in his country soccer is the national sport. He said he'd give me all kinds of pointers. Jose's now studying to be an ambulance driver. He only needs to finish one more course and he'll be ready. I feel good that Jose will be out there driving around in an ambulance. Who knows if I'll ever need to go to the hospital? If I do, I know he'll drive fast and make sure I'm still breathing.

I met Courtney at our lockers, which are, of course, right next to each other. She couldn't believe I didn't bring my soccer shoes to school. I tried to explain to her that I never thought I would make the team.

After we put on our PE clothes we went outside. All the Losers except me were gone, and of course so was the Super Loser. Everyone looked sort of surprised to see me. Courtney stayed at my side like a guard dog, so no one said anything.

When we got out onto the field Otto was waiting. Otto wanted to talk to us about what position we each were interested in playing. I figured my position would be on the bench. But he wanted to know if we saw ourselves as offensive players or defensive. Courtney whispered to me to say 'defense,' which I did. We then did all kinds of drills. We ran back and forth across the field, touching the ground at each end. He called them "wind sprints." It felt like they were designed to kill you.

I could pretty much keep up with everyone even though I had on regular shoes. I don't have muscular legs, but I weigh a lot less than the other girls. While we were catching our breath from running around, Otto talked about nutrition. He said it was really important that we eat right. Breakfast is really a big deal to him. I didn't volunteer that I always have instant coffee and a plate of small marshmallows. He said we needed to drink water all day and eat carbohydrates before big games. He said our parents know good food from junk food, and to eat green vegetables.

Obviously he doesn't know about my Nammy. I can't even remember the last time she made a meal for me. Besides, her idea of green vegetables is hot dog relish, which I don't even like. I was hoping that celery was a big deal to him but he didn't bring it up.

After the food talk he said a bunch of stuff about being a team and sticking together and using each other's talents. He told us that we were all there for a reason and we each had something special to offer. I caught a couple girls looking at me weird. I just ignored it because I'm used to that kind of thing.

It was starting to get dark when he said we were done. I was so tired I couldn't believe it. My hair was all sweaty and my face was red. Courtney didn't even look like she'd done anything. She spent the whole practice watching Otto and listening to him. Like there was a secret message in everything he said and she only had a few minutes to figure it out or we'd all be blown up. We turned back to the gym when Otto called my name. "Sasha, can I speak to you?"

It was the moment I'd been waiting for. He was going to tell me that somehow he'd mixed me up with someone else. He had written down the wrong name and hoped I understood that he was a foreigner and didn't mean anything by it. I just looked at him, waiting for the speech.

"You're new to soccer."

I nodded my head.

"I think you have a lot of potential."

When someone says that you have a lot of potential it means you're really bad.

I nodded again.

"I've been thinking, and I figure goalie might

be a good place for you."

The way he said this made me feel like I was a piece of furniture someone made him take that he hated and he just realized he could put it in the garage. I just stared at him. Being the goalie is the scariest thing you can do on a soccer field. Balls are kicked at incredible speeds. You are supposed to on purpose throw yourself in front of them. My whole body went stiff.

"Madeline Bingham is our goalie."

Now he was nodding.

"You're right. But we'll need a back-up."

I just looked at him blankly. I said, "I think Shawna Sully wants to be the back-up."

He nodded again. "Yes. But we'll need a back-up to the back-up."

A back-up to a back-up. It was perfect. I wouldn't get near the ball in a real game. I smiled: "It sounds good."

And I meant it. He was smiling now, too. His smile was all white teeth. If he told me to run onto the highway and stop traffic, I'd do it.

He winked at me as he said, "It's settled then."

EIGHTEEN

We practiced every day after school for the first week. By Friday I had blisters all over my feet and was limping. I couldn't believe how much we had to run. Around the field and then across it. We ran diagonally and in circles a million times. The grass looked as flat and worn as an old green rug.

I was now exhausted all the time. And hungry. Mostly I never have much of an appetite. Nammy has always called me the world's pickiest eater. I'd rather have little pains in my stomach than swallow something that smells weird. But after a few soccer practices I added a piece of toast to my breakfast. And I started eating lunch. Normally I'd just sit with Courtney while she ate her peanut butter sandwich. I'd always qualified for a free hot lunch, but never bothered to pick it up. Now I did.

A lot of things in the hot lunch line freak me out. Every day there's mystery meat, which swims in a thick gray sauce. It smells like the dead leaves on the street that pile up in the gutter. I couldn't even look at it. In the next tray was rice or noodles, and then some kind of potato dish. This is followed by a big section of steamed vegetables. I swear they put out the same ones every day because I've never seen one kid take any. After the display-only broccoli and carrots, the few things I would consider swallowing began. There is Jell-O, canned fruit, cottage cheese, and bread products.

I started eating a canned peach, saltine crackers and a little container of peanuts. Courtney was real happy that I was eating something during the day. She said it was a start.

Having Nammy as my "parents" has probably affected me a lot in the food department. She eats the grossest things. Her favorite meal is pickled herring in sour cream. It looks like snakes in a jar. She also loves really smelly cheese and anything with hot sauce or clumps of garlic. She puts all kinds of things together that weren't meant to be paired. Like scrambled eggs and tuna fish fried with a can of chili. Nammy will pretty much eat anything.

NINETEEN

After two weeks of Otto's conditioning we were ready to pay attention to the game. Courtney was our center mid-fielder and on special occasions would play forward. The other girls were sprinkled around the field. It depended on whether they had speed or a good kick or some other skill. I still didn't really understand the game even though it wasn't that complicated. You want to kick the ball into the other side's net. When you do everyone cheers and you get a point. When they kick it into your net everyone gets mad and they get the point. And even though you can do good things on your own, you need the rest of the players to make any of it work, so it's really a team sport which is kind of nice.

At practice, Madeline Bingham was one goalie and Shawna Sully took the other side. That left me to chase after balls and generally hang out near Otto. Madeline and Shawna did their best to include me when we did our goalie drills. But I didn't like anyone kicking the ball at me, so my practice was limited.

Madeline told me she never wanted to be a goalie but some coach made her when she was little. She was tall and he thought she'd be able to reach farther to stop balls. After that, everyone thought of her as a goalie. They expected her to do it, and she couldn't get out of it after that.

That's why it's important not to go to dental school unless you really want to be a dentist. Once people see you there, they get it in their heads that's what you do. But how are you supposed to know what you want until you've tried? That's the problem in a lot of things that grown-ups have to face. You could start doing something and maybe you don't even care about it. But then you realize a ton of time later you're trapped in it for life. That's why I will never, ever work in a funeral parlor. I know I'd get stuck there forever.

Even though Madeline doesn't like being a goalie, she's so good because she's not afraid. She just wants the ball to hit her. She'll dive straight out, hit the dirt hard, and never cries or even complains. She's real tough like a boy, which is funny because when she's not on the field she only talks about going shopping for new clothes and lip gloss. That's one of the things I like about the team. It's full of surprises.

Shawna Sully, who is our back-up goalie, is one of them. Shawna is good, but just not as good as Madeline. She hasn't done it as long, and she gets nervous and sort of falls apart. You can tell Shawna is always thinking about ten things at the same time. She'll be looking at where the ball is and then hear something or see something. She'll get distracted and she won't know what's going on. I try to be encouraging to her because I really think that she's brave. It's not easy to go do the job when you aren't naturally talented like Madeline.

The good news for me is that I have them both there to play. Everyone knows I don't need to worry about ever taking the field. But I still feel like part of the team. I run the laps and chase the balls like anyone else. Otto also says I'm good at seeing little things. I watch for him to see if Nicole Parada is turning her foot out right. Or if Helen Herlihy is going off-sides when no one's watching. She can't help herself. She gets excited and runs so fast she just goes right by the defender.

My life had a new routine. I stayed after school to practice and then Mr. Bilsesser drove us home. He usually had some kind of treat in the car for us, which was good. He also always asked a lot of boring questions, which was bad.

Everyone thought our team would do well because we had a lot of talent. They didn't mean me of course, but I'm still happy to hear them say that.

Eleanor Roosevelt's mascot is the Eagle. I don't know why. I don't think Eleanor Roosevelt had anything to do with eagles. Maybe it's because she liked them a lot or something.

So we were the Eagles and I was part of a group. My last group had been the 'Campfire Girls' which is little Girl Scouts. I quit 'Campfire Girls' after only three weeks. Nammy didn't think it was a good thing to learn about starting fires even though I told her a bunch of times that wasn't part of it. But I was okay with quitting. I was afraid in the big, dark auditorium where we had to meet. Nobody was interested when I said we should find a new headquarters.

That's one good thing about a soccer field. I didn't have to worry about anyone sneaking up on me.

TWENTY

Otto asked us to wear our uniforms to school the day of our first game. It was weird for me because I've never done anything like that before. I swear it felt like the whole school was staring at me. Courtney's worn all kinds of uniforms and didn't think a thing about it. When Nammy saw me in my uniform, she said I looked like a grasshopper. I think that's because I have long, thin legs and I was squatting down.

Since I'm technically a goalie, I also have a long-sleeve shirt. But I put that away in my locker and didn't wear it. I think it's only right for Madeline to walk around in that goalie shirt. When Otto handed out the uniforms I thought it was a good time to give my speech about maybe wearing helmets or other protective gear. Everyone just laughed like I was making a big joke so I had to pretend that I was. But I think

Otto could tell I was serious because he looked at me real strange.

Everyone still thinks Otto's the hottest guy they've ever seen. But we've gotten used to him now so it's not such a big deal. We've seen him burp and blow his nose and stick his finger in his ear and poke around for earwax. Plus we've all talked to him a lot so he's become about half human. We still feel sort of light-headed around him, but at least we can breathe.

I remember in second grade when this new girl came to our school. Her name was Hilly Saunders, and she had a big purplish patch on her face the size of a muffin. It was some kind of birthmark. When I first saw her I couldn't believe how strange she looked. A few of the mean boys nicknamed her 'Inky' because it looked like someone spilled ink on her and it never got cleaned up. When I talked to Hilly I wasn't sure if I should look at the purple spot or not look at the purple spot. I ended up mostly looking right past her left ear, which was as far away from the purple spot as my eyes could get. But then after awhile of seeing her every day, she didn't look weird anymore. I guess I got used to it. And it wasn't just me. The mean boys stopped calling her 'Inky.' She was just Hilly who was good at kickball and had four hamsters. I guess it's kind of like Robbie Ellis having those really big ears. After awhile, who even notices?

So it was kind of that way with Otto, only in reverse. He was still incredible looking. If the sun was going down and he was standing in front of it so that his head of curls was kind of glowing, it still felt like a spiritual experience or something. But otherwise he was the guy with the clipboard telling us to try harder.

It's funny how you can do way more in a group than you'd ever do on your own. I would never in a million, trillion years go run around our field twelve times. But by the time our first game arrived we'd been doing it a lot. At first I got side aches and thought my legs were going to fall off. After awhile I knew I'd live and then it just got sort of boring.

Then came the actual game. When we ran out to the field, there were parents and kids waiting to watch. Courtney's mom couldn't get away from work but her dad came. He brought juice boxes and protein bars and was all excited. He came over and told me he knew I'd do great. I smiled. I didn't tell him I wouldn't be playing, which was just the way I wanted it.

The team we played was from across town and came in a bus. The girls looked around like they couldn't believe what a dump our school was. That was insulting, considering their bus didn't look so hot. Then their player, number six, took the field and used her elbow as a weapon. She held onto jerseys when she thought the referee wasn't looking. She pretended to trip so she could knock into one of our players and send them to the ground with her.

I'd never seen anything like it. All of the sudden

the game looked even more violent and dangerous. From the safety of Otto's side I watched with my mouth open. I was stunned. Fortunately most of our team played as if it was no big deal. At half time we were ahead one to nothing. Helen Herlihy had scored on Courtney's perfectly placed corner kick. Otto then made a bunch of adjustments during the break. We were now playing with another forward up front and fewer mid-fielders.

Otto had assigned me to keep track of statistics. I had to write down when someone took a shot on goal, who made the assists, when Madeline made a save and a bunch of other stuff. It kept me really busy. It also made me realize what was going on. The other team had two strong players who were the best on their team. We had Courtney, and four other players who were as good as their two stars. It all caught up to them even with their number six practically biting our players. We pulled ahead four to zero.

Even though I didn't play, I couldn't believe how happy I was that we'd won. I ran out onto the field with Otto and the other substitute players. We all were jumping up and down and kind of making really shrieky noises which normally I would have hated.

It wasn't until then that I saw Nammy sitting in a lawn chair. She was on our side of the field, down by the end. She was in a pink and gold jumpsuit, wearing her black "Cher" wig. She'd given it a haircut so it was now shoulder length. It didn't look half as loony as it did when I left the house.

When she saw me she started cheering like I'd won the Olympics.

You just have to love Nammy.

TWENTY-ONE

After that first match, Nammy was a real fan. She put her heart and soul into the idea of soccer. She started watching the Spanish language channel to catch matches. And pretty soon everything she was wearing was in our colors. She ordered a gob of new athletic sweaters she saw on TV. She even found an old felt St. Patrick's Day hat with an eagle on it. It was from her second husband Kirby who was Irish and liked to sing late at night. She still had a ton of his things even though they'd been divorced forever. He could've come and got the stuff if he wanted to, but he never did.

We had an electric rock polisher that belonged to Kirby. It made such a racket when it was on you thought you were going to scream just listening to that thing rumble. I used to bring rocks home and then load them up in the polisher. I let the rocks roll around in there for hours. They made the kind of noise a metal zipper in the dryer makes, only about a million times worse. I always thought one of the rocks would turn out to have a diamond in it. Me and Nammy would then be rich. She could order anything she wanted on TV and I could get the home security system with the moving cameras and the twenty-four hour surveillance that I always dreamed about.

But the closest I came was a rock that was dark green when I had finished polishing it. For awhile I thought I had something but I got a book out of the public library and it turned out to be some kind of common ore that all the mountains are made of around here. I still felt it was special so I figured it was magic. I'd make wishes on the rock but I was careful always to wish on things that I couldn't check up on, like starving kids who lived in tents suddenly finding peanut butter sandwiches and jelly beans on their pillows in the morning.

Once soccer season started I took the rock with me to school every game day. I didn't tell anyone because it would be one more thing they didn't understand. I also believe that magic is more powerful when no one knows.

With the help of the rock and Courtney we won our second game. Everyone was surprised because the team from Jefferson always was really good. Courtney made two of our four goals and already was leading the league in scoring. They kept track of our league on the internet so we could see the statistics. I checked a few times a day even though I knew things couldn't change. I'm like that sometimes, like if I boil something on the stove. I have to check about ten times to make sure I turned off the stove. I read in a book that this might mean that later I could go crazy. But I'm still a kid, so I'm hoping it just means I'm careful.

In the second game Alexandra Leon hurt herself. She and this other girl from Jefferson were pushing and shoving each other. They were both yelled at, and then the referee decided to do a "drop ball." I think a drop ball is just a plain bad idea. And after what happened, I know Alexandra thinks so, too. They stood facing each other and then the referee dropped the ball in between them. Alexandra took a huge step forward and put her whole body into her kick. So did the girl from Jefferson. Unfortunately they both missed and ended up kicking each other right in the foot.

They had to carry Alexandra off the field and she couldn't stop crying. The other girl walked off with her coach and her mother on either side. Alexandra had a fracture in her foot and they put her in a cast. I asked her about ten times to see her x-rays, but she never brought them.

So Alexandra was out for the season. She was real good about it though, and we all signed her cast. Then a lot of the boys in our grade got interested in the sport. They realized we must be playing hard if one of us could break a bone. After that a group of the cool boys came to all our games. They traveled in a pack, jumping up on top of each other a lot. They didn't stand around and plot and plan like the girls. They were always chasing each other and hitting and making noise. Even the ones with a brain got all nuts when they were in a group.

Having the boys around made it hard for some of the girls to concentrate. This made Otto really upset, and so he made a rule. During a game, we couldn't look behind us at the bleachers. If someone did, she had to run a lap around the field after the game. Amber Rizzo didn't care and ended up running at least two laps after every match. She also had her mother tailor her uniform shorts to make them fit tighter.

I didn't have a problem with her even though the first time she saw Nammy in her lawn chair on the sidelines she went crazy laughing. Courtney took her by the arm and went off far enough that I couldn't hear. I don't know what she told her but after that Amber only smiled at me. She even offered to give me a beauty makeover if I ever wanted one.

I told her I was always really busy, which was a lie. I also said that I lived with a registered beautician, which was true. Nammy was trained to do a lot of things she didn't end up doing. It's what made her so good at doing crossword puzzles.

TWENTY-TWO

We won our third game and everyone started talking about an undefeated season. The kids in art class painted big signs with Eagles kicking soccer balls. Then the drill team did a dance for us at an assembly. All of a sudden it was like the whole school was be-hind the team. Of course, we then went out and lost our next game. I felt it coming. We were playing Franklin Middle School. And Ashley Aiken was their Captain.

I hadn't seen much of Ashley since I'd started soccer. Since Mr. Bilsesser always drove us home, I didn't have to avoid passing her house. But we'd all heard that the other good girls' middle school soccer team was Franklin. So I can't say I hadn't thought about her.

The way our league works is that we play every team twice. The team with the best record in the end is the champion. So far, neither one of us had ever lost a game.

Otto gave us a talk about playing hard and focusing and not getting too excited. The truth is, we were too at Shawna Scully because Shawna said she'd sit with her. The problem was, Shawna told Drina Archer the same thing. Shawna didn't think it was a big deal but Amber did. Then Drina got really mad at Amber even though Amber was just mad at Shawna. Rosie Chung got involved when she got up and sat next to Drina. Amber yelled at Rosie, which was really not right. Then Madeline got mad at Amber because she's really good friends with Rosie and couldn't stand to see her upset. Pretty soon everyone had an idea about who was to blame and started fighting. When we got off the bus, half the team wasn't speaking to the other half.

That's not a good way to start a big game. We tried to make up during warm-ups, but it wasn't happening. I think it was nerves that got the fight going to begin with.

Franklin Middle School is scary. See, our school looks like a school. It's made of old brown bricks and has a ratty hedge growing around it. Franklin looks like a hospital or a factory or something. The buildings are new and made of glass and metal. Everything looks sharp, like it could shatter and hurt you. That's how it looked to me anyway. They also aren't stuck with old, gray wooden bleachers on the sidelines. Instead, they have shiny metal seats and a real electric scoreboard with lights and everything.

We acted like it was no big deal but we were all impressed. The only thing we had that got their attention was Otto. I saw the way the Franklin girls looked at him. They were talking and laughing and then they shut up right away and just stared. Their coach was a woman who must have been in the army before. She barked orders so loud her face turned real red. And she didn't look at Otto even once, which is just so wrong.

Ashley and I saw each other right away, and of course she laughed. She pointed me out to a few of her teammates, and I just looked away. I told Courtney. She nodded in a way that said she got it.

Courtney plays 'center-mid,' which is short for the center mid-fielder. This is the player who works to control the game because everything goes through them. They run the distance from goal to goal, sometimes on every play. They have to have speed, a big kick, and the ability to control the ball. But Otto says that true soccer players have another thing as well. He says they can see the field while they are playing. Eventually I realized what he meant. You have to see what's happening where the ball *isn't*. You know what's ahead. You're thinking about where the ball could go and who could be there. And you're doing that while you're running down the field to do something about it.

Not many players can really see the field, and it

takes all kinds of experience. Otto says it requires this other thing that you're either born with or you're not. Nammy says I was born with a fever and a rash all over my body. It took forceps and a suction cup and loads of medicine to get me out.

I guess I've always been afraid of the unknown.

TWENTY-THREE

So we started out slow and just never caught up. Ashley Aiken was their center-mid and so she lined up across from Courtney. Then she said something that made Courtney's face squeeze up.

They scored in the first five minutes and after that we were stuck playing catch-up. We were always a goal behind until the end, when they won four to three.

On the bus ride home Madeline cried. She felt like it was all her fault since she was the goalie. Amber and Drina and Shawna completely put aside their fighting and sat by her. Courtney was silent all the way back. She'd scored two goals and should have felt good about that but she didn't. We didn't win, and that was all that mattered to her. She just looked out the window the whole ride. I knew she was replaying the game in her head, so I didn't say anything.

Before we got off the bus, Otto stood up to say something. I thought he was going to tell us to not feel bad. You know, because we'd tried hard and everything. But he didn't. He said we had to do better. He said we had to try harder, that Franklin's team was tougher, mentally and physically. He said he was disappointed in us, and he was disappointed in himself.

I could hear my heart pounding in my chest when he finished. I knew that meant my blood pressure was really high, and I immediately started worrying. I was going to have a heart attack and croak right there on the bus. My face was burning and my hair was all sticky with sweat. I thought for sure I was going to throw up, but luckily I didn't.

Courtney and I got off the bus and found our backpacks in the gym. She still wasn't talking so I just followed silently by her side. Mr. Bilsesser said right away in the car that Courtney had played a great game. She just acted like she couldn't hear him and looked out the window again.

That's when I realized she was what they call a 'true competitor.' All the other girls felt bad after we lost and real crummy after Otto's speech. But I could see them all talking and laughing going to their cars. They were already over it and thinking about what was for dinner and stuff. But not Courtney. When she lost it hurt deep inside. I wanted to say it was only a game and that it didn't matter. But I could tell she didn't feel that way.

When we arrived at my house and I said goodbye to Courtney, all of a sudden I got it. I could tell by the way her jaw looked that she was grinding her teeth. Courtney didn't really care that much about soccer. She didn't care about being first in the league or being the most valuable player. She cared about Otto and she felt she had let him down.

When I got in the house I made a plate of celery and peanut butter. I sat down next to Nammy in front of the TV, watching the weather channel. I was just thinking about Courtney and trying to figure it out. I decided that sometimes you could want things and do things more for someone else than for yourself. She was playing so hard for Otto and she probably didn't even know it. All of a sudden I could see why people fought wars and jumped out of airplanes and did all kinds of wacky stuff. They had something else, maybe a person, floating around in their heads, and that changed the way they saw the world.

I went into my room and got out Mom's old trunk. I kept a little notebook there where I recorded really, really, really important things. They were only for me to see, and I never wanted to forget them. I think I got in the habit of doing this because I don't have parents. Maybe if you have them they can just tell you these kinds of things. I wrote down that it was possible to make yourself better for someone else. I then wrote alongside this that you could be faster and stronger, too. I wasn't sure if you could be braver, but I thought about it. After awhile I decided that it was possible.

The last time I'd written in the notebook, I wrote that all people are gray. They weren't all good, or all bad. They were in the middle. Who they were was all about different shades. Finding this out helped when strange things happened. Like the time some man yelled at me to get off his sidewalk. I know that the sidewalk is owned by the city and not by him. I found out later that a car had hit his dog that morning. He was outside yelling at everyone all day.

I tried to tell myself that even awful Ashley Aiken had something good about her. Maybe she once helped an old lady across the street, but I really doubted it.

Her team was better than we were, at least that afternoon. I just hoped for Courtney's sake it wouldn't stay that way.

TWENTY-FOUR

After that first loss our practices were a lot harder. We ran more and stayed on the field longer. We were all anxious now for our next game. We wanted to show Otto and the world how seriously we were taking this. We were playing Lincoln, who weren't very good, so we were feeling pretty good already.

The thing about sports is that the big unknown is whether someone will get hurt. I'm always looking for ways you can hurt yourself, like falling objects and slippery surfaces. I wasn't thinking someone in a uniform could attack you.

That's what happened to Madeline. We were already up by two and the other team was really frustrated, I guess. At least number ten was, a big girl who had thick legs like trees. Madeline had come out of the goalie box to get the ball. She was fearless, diving straight at the ball, but number ten didn't care. She flung her foot back and kicked as hard as she could.

What would have been the ball turned out to be Madeline's knee.

You could tell right away it was bad. Madeline cried out in pain like she'd been shot. She landed on the ground and she grabbed onto her knee in agony. I couldn't see her face because it was stuck into the grass and dirt. I took off along with Otto and we both ran out onto the field.

Chelsea Luzzato's grandfather was there and he's a doctor. Otto looked up with a face that said Madeline was really messed up. Some of the boys ran back to the gym and got a stretcher. Madeline got loaded up and was carried off by a bunch of people. We were supposed to resume play, but we had our eyes glued on the stretcher. Their number ten got a yellow card and was now sitting on the sidelines crying. The ref placed the ball down and we got a free kick. Amber scored but nobody cared, even Otto, who always goes crazy after a goal.

Shawna Sully went in as goalie and did a good job. We won five to two but no one was celebrating. Madeline's leg was going to be in a cast for two months. Nammy had come late to the game and missed the whole thing. We all told her what happened and she just couldn't believe it. Her questions were about Madeline's health insurance and who would pay for all the costs. Mr. Bilsesser kept saying it wouldn't be a problem but Nammy didn't believe him.

It wasn't until we were home that I realized I

was now the back-up goalie. Before I'd been the back-up to the back-up, which was very safe. Now it was possible I might have to actually play. Shawna usually came in near the end if we were winning. A few times Madeline had even gone out to be a forward or a midfielder.

Just thinking about my new responsibilities made me feel sick. I took my temperature three times but I didn't have a fever. I felt all hot and sweaty so this was hard to believe.

I lay in bed for hours staring at the ceiling. I only fell asleep after I decided to talk to Otto about changing positions. If he wouldn't let me, I would jump off our roof and into the front yard. I'd break my legs for sure and everything would be okay.

TWENTY-FIVE

Madeline was back the next day, and we all sat with her in the cafeteria. We told the story of how she got hurt but I had the official version. I could remember the little things, like number ten had earrings with ladybugs on them. Girls like Mona Baron got too excited and just went right to the injury part.

Madeline was really sad about missing the rest of the season. She really loved the sport and looked forward to it all year long. But her life wasn't all rotten now. Her dad got her a whole new video game system which she'd really wanted. And her big sister had to switch rooms with her because Madeline's bedroom was upstairs. The big sister's room had its own bathroom and was right next to the kitchen. Madeline hoped her sister would go off to college and she'd have it for real. Helen Herlihy told her to keep limping, complain about the stairs and it might happen.

After classes, I went straight out to the field to discuss my plan with Otto. He cut me off right away and told me to go get dressed. He said I was a goalie and halfway through the season there was no turning back. I thought about sneaking off back home but when I saw everyone else I couldn't. Madeline was on her crutches with the rest of the team. She wanted to watch us practice and she smiled big when she saw me. She said she was giving me her goalie shirt. The last thing I wanted to do was to wear it but I acted like I was happy. Courtney made me put the thing on, and of course it was way too big. On my body it looked like a dress.

But the worst part was yet to come. After we ran around for awhile Otto had us scrimmage. The two goalies weren't Madeline and Shawna anymore. They were me and Shawna. I went straight to Courtney. I didn't have to say anything because she saw how pale I was, and how my hands were trembling. They were like Nammy's hands when she tries to thread a needle. Courtney whispered that she'd make sure no ball would get anywhere near my goal. I could tell she meant it and so I stopped breathing so funny.

I tried to figure out how I'd ended up in this mess. I had all these people now counting on me to do something that was just plain against my natural instincts. What sane person wants to throw their body in the path of a soccer ball? It was just ridiculous.

Otto blew his whistle and Courtney was true to her word. She scrambled around the field, making sure no one got a shot at my net. She played as if her life depended on it. At first I just stared out at the game in rigid fear. But whenever the ball came near me, I started yelling like crazy to my teammates. I was telling them where to go, and what to do to get the ball. I shouted so much that at the end, I had almost completely lost my voice. Only when Otto started to laugh did I realize how crazy I must have sounded.

It turned out that they'd never taken a shot on goal on me. Mostly this was because of Courtney, but according to Otto that wasn't the only reason. Otto gave a speech about the importance of communication on the field. He said how great it was that I was back there hollering my head off. I saw Madeline stare down at the ground for just a second. She was always quiet when she played and she must have felt sad about it. Then I realized Shawna Sully was chewing on her thumbnail and looking worried. That's when I realized I was in real trouble.

Instead of showing them all what a loser I was, I'd supposedly taught them something. I couldn't believe it. On top of everything else, Courtney looked as happy as I'd ever seen her. Otto took her aside and told her what a great job she'd done. Her face turned all red and she just smiled and smiled.

I thought again about how I'd been tricked into this whole thing. I never liked soccer and now I could boot one almost half-way across the field. I've never liked to run and now I could run a lot without breathing different. I was eating more, sleeping less, and I had more energy. And there was nothing I could do about it.

I'd completely lost control of my own life.

TWENTY-SIX

A week later we had our next game. I was up almost the whole night worrying about everything from hunger in central Africa to whether termites were eating the foundation of Nammy's house and causing terrible damage to what was already not a stable structure. I wouldn't allow myself to even think about soccer. I knew I'd be breathing into a paper bag covered with cold sweat if I did.

As it turned out I didn't have anything to worry about. Shawna Sully played the whole game and we won three to nothing. Nammy showed up with her lawn chair and a big "Go Eagles" sign. She'd cut her black wig shorter again and she was starting to look more normal. Either that or I was just getting used to her with straight synthetic hair.

Courtney had a great game and scored two of

the three goals. And Shawna yelled at our team throughout the game to get in position. Otto was very happy when it was all over. He gathered us around and told each of us what we'd contributed to the victory. I was thinking my big contribution was the fact that I didn't play. He had other ideas. He said that my courage in the face of Madeline's injury had been an inspiration to the team. And then on behalf of the team he thanked me.

No one on the planet has ever called me courageous. In kindergarten, I refused all year to go up the stairs to the library. I failed beginning swimming class because I wouldn't move out of the shallow end. Plus I've called 911 so often that I know two operators by their first names. I'm afraid to even count all of my fears because I know I'll freak out.

But Otto wasn't kidding. He meant it about my being courageous. And I don't think it was because he was a foreigner and misunderstood me. He really thought I somehow had helped my teammates. Go figure.

Having someone call you something can make you feel more that way. I guess that's why it's important to not call a chubby kid 'Fatso.' You just keep them in that condition. But the opposite is true, too. If you tell someone they are something good, they can be more of it. I started to feel like I wasn't the biggest chicken on the planet. It was kind of like the Cowardly Lion in "The Wizard of Oz." Otto gave me my courage.

Which isn't to say I was now patrolling the neighborhood looking for bad guys. Nor was I killing the spiders in the bathroom. But I didn't feel like jumping out of my own skin as much as usual.

And then I used the same approach with Nammy. She'd bought some orange dye for the living room curtains, to brighten up the place. They were once white and now were really faded and kind of old and dirty. She loaded them into the washing machine, which was where she decided to dye them.

I think if you do that, you're supposed to take them out right away. But Nammy was watching some program where people cook food while dressed up as farm animals. When she finally unloaded the curtains they'd been in for a few hours. She yelled for me and I could see right away that it didn't work right. The orange dye had stuck only in spots. They looked like something you'd see in the window of a hippie van that had been driving around for a million years and parking in the sun. Also, the fabric wasn't strong enough to take the violence of a washing machine. Tons of thread had come undone like a million cats had clawed it.

Nammy stared at the curtains. But before she could say anything I shrieked about how great they now were. I said they looked so cool with all the different shades of orange and the loose strings dangling. I said no one would ever be able to duplicate the look. It was so original. So modern. Nammy looked at me and then at the curtains and then back at me. I was smiling big and running my hand over the wrecked material.

Suddenly Nammy started smiling, too. She looked right at me, "You really like them?"

I nodded. "Oh yeah. They look tie-dyed!"

Nammy nodded now, too. "Yeah. That's kind of what I was going after."

We put them up together which was harder than taking them down. I even climbed up onto a ladder which I hate to do. When I finally got off, Nammy was admiring the new look, pleased as could be. She gushed, "They're original, that's for sure!"

I was so glad to see that she was happy. I didn't even care that it looked like a tiger lived in the house.

I slipped my hand into hers and I meant it when I said, "Who'd want it any other way?"

TWENTY-SEVEN

We practiced all the next week in the rain, and we paid the price. Half the team ended up with colds, coughing up really gross-colored stuff. Anyone would have picked me to get sick first, but I felt totally normal. Courtney went through the whole third grade without missing a day of school and got a special prize and everything. Now even she didn't feel well.

There were only three games left and so Otto told us all kinds of stories. They were of people he knew in Hungary who played under any condition. They had intense fevers and broken legs and all kinds of other health problems. He was trying to be inspirational but he made me think that these people were crazy. He knew people who got up out of hospital beds to play soccer. We have all kinds of rules at school about our health. If you haven't been to class during the day, you can't play in after-school sports.

Unbelievably, on game day everyone on our

team was there in the morning. Rosie Chung took so much cold medicine she fell asleep in second period. The nurse sent her home so we knew we didn't have our regular left fullback. After lunch, three other girls were in the office calling their parents. Amber Rizzo had a sore throat and Helen Herlihy had thrown up in history. Chelsea Luzzato coughed so much the science teacher made her leave. I felt bad for them but all I really cared about was Shawna Sully. She had an awful cold but there was nothing else wrong with her. I brought her orange juice from the snack bar just in case. If nothing else, I was hoping I'd catch whatever she had. Then there would be no question of ever putting me in the game.

But I continued to feel fine and she felt worse as the day wore on. Shawna blew her nose about a million times on the bus to the game. Fortunately Otto wasn't feeling very well by this point so he didn't seem to notice.

Otto had us go really easy during our warmups. Half the team would go into coughing fits if they started breathing hard. I faked a few sneezes but no one paid any attention. The first half went by without a problem and we led two to one. Shawna didn't look so great but neither did anyone else, really. Courtney wasn't playing like she used to, either. She twice apologized about it to Otto, who just told her to do her best.

We had about eight minutes left when Shawna's

face suddenly turned all red. She looked like a fish that had flopped out of its tank. Her mouth was open and she was gasping for air. I noticed right away because I had my eyes on her the whole time. At first I hoped she'd settle down, but then I realized something was really wrong. I ran over to Otto and pointed her out. Right when I did this Shawna fell to her knees. Courtney purposely kicked the ball out of bounds so Otto could get the ref's attention. The ref stopped the clock and let Otto go out onto the field. At this point Shawna was all curled up like a pill bug.

That's when I found out that Shawna had asthma. Her mother showed up out of nowhere and was on the field with an inhaler. The truth was, half our team was now having trouble breathing. The next part happened so fast I wasn't sure what was going on. Shawna came off the field sort of propped up by Otto and the ref. She leaned way more on Otto than on the old ref. I was hoping she would remember what his strong Hungarian shoulder felt like. Once she was on the bench, they got her goalie shirt off. Then Otto pulled it over my head and pushed me out onto the field.

Until now, it didn't seem that the other team's girls even cared about the sport. But once they put me in they must have sensed they had a chance. Out of nowhere they came alive and gained control of the ball. I watched helplessly as they charged as a team straight down towards me. I started yelling as if my life depended on it, and Courtney went after the ball. But the rest of the team was too tired and sick to really follow instructions. It looked to me like they were all moving in slow motion.

But the ball wasn't. Their fastest forward went right past our sweeper and crossed to the middle. Courtney sprinted but she couldn't get there soon enough. I watched in horror as their strongest player took a shot. Once the ball connected with her foot I instinctively dove out of the way.

As luck would have it, her kick had some top-spin. Instead of going straight, it curved over and hit the back of my extended legs. By trying to get out of the way I'd made a save. Once the ball hit me I fell on top of it immediately. When I got up I saw Otto on the sidelines cheering. Even though Shawna had her inhaler in her mouth she was pumping her fist.

The last thing I wanted was to put the ball back in play but I had to. Fortunately I can kick the thing, and I cleared it out to the other side. I could tell by Courtney's face that she'd keep the ball away no matter what. She tripped a girl who had the ball and I knew she wasn't even sorry. When the game ended, I still couldn't believe I was actually on the field playing. I was still looking out in horror as if the other team was still coming at me. Not until Courtney came running over to me did I really believe it was over.

Everyone started hugging me; Shawna and Otto hugged me the hardest out of everyone. Then as we headed to the sidelines it started to rain. It was good because I was sort of crying and now you couldn't tell the raindrops from my tears. But it was more than that. I decided to stand there, letting the rain pour on me. I stuck my palms out and the water soaked me through and through. It felt good. Courtney came running over, looking concerned. Then we looked at each other. We both laughed at the same time, and then ran into the gym.

I'd played in a soccer game.

TWENTY-EIGHT

Shawna was feeling okay for our next game and she played the whole time. We won without a problem, and that left only one game in the season. It was against Franklin Middle School and the dreaded Ashley Aiken. Since the only time we'd lost was to Franklin, we had a lot to prove. They had the same record as us—eight wins and one loss. Whoever won this game would end the season with the best record in the league. If we won, we'd be making school history. For the first time in twenty years, our school would finish with the best record.

Of course, Otto thought we could do it. By now, most of the girls were feeling better, and Shawna had a new inhaler. I was also okay now being the goalie in our scrimmages. Most of the time I still ducked or jumped out of the way, which is exactly what I was not supposed to do. But every now and then I actually blocked a shot. Plus, I could kick the ball pretty far, so I wasn't a total loser. I was also always yelling my head off, and then everyone started yelling. This turned out to be a good thing, at least according to Otto.

This time, the game against Franklin was at our school. When I got up that morning, I was in for a big surprise. Nammy had made me pancakes with chocolate chips inside. I couldn't remember her ever making pancakes my whole life, and certainly not this early. I didn't even have to pretend they tasted great because they really did. After I ate, she went back to bed because she's not a morning person. But first she blew me a kiss goodbye and said she was proud of me.

At school everyone knew this was our big game day. The cool boys even came over and talked to us before our first class. They always tried to talk to Courtney but now they were talking to all of us. Stephen Boyd leaned against my locker and asked me a few soccer questions. I got all nervous because he always made me feel that way. Stephen was smart and cool, which wasn't normally the way it worked. He wasn't very tall but had big brown eyes. They made it impossible for me to look at him because I got this weird feeling in my stomach when I did. So I didn't look at him or answer any of his questions and he finally got the message and headed off to math class. After he was gone I got really mad at myself. He probably now knew I liked him since I wouldn't talk to him.

We all sat together at lunch and tried not to think about the game. We mostly concentrated on Otto. He was going back to Europe in two months and we all felt sick about it. Courtney had been reading up on Hungary and it was amazing how much she knew about the place. We were all shocked when she told us that she had memorized a few sayings. She taught us to say "Nagyon szepen koszonom, kocsi." In Hungarian that means, "Thank you so much, coach." After awhile it became a chant and we were yelling it like crazy. We were so loud that Mr. Edelman came and told us to keep it down.

More people showed up for this game than ever before. Courtney's dad was there like always, but this time her mom came, too. And her brothers Ned and Wally walked over from the high school to watch. Jose was standing on the sidelines and he called out my name, waving to me. I hadn't seen him since he left school and got the job in the ambulance. I was really happy to see him in his new uniform.

Ms. Biculos came in her high heels and one of her totally impractical tight skirts. The principal, Mr. Hockstatter, showed up a few minutes later. He went and sat with Ms. Biculos in the bleachers. Coach Moshofsky brought out a big cooler of water, which was nice. She smiled at me and said good luck and I could tell she meant it. We'd gotten to be friends after the deal we made during basketball season. Jessica Pendergast was there with a bunch of girls from the drill team. She was the girl I'd tripped during basketball try-outs. She was done with physical therapy and really happy to be out of her brace. She gave us all a wave and shouted "Go Eagles." The cool boys all came together in a herd like a group of livestock. I saw Stephen Boyd in the center of the pack. They sat up on the top of the bleachers all in a row. I thought that they looked like birds on an electrical wire.

Even my and Courtney's advisor, Mrs. Wiener, stayed after school for the game. She always got everything wrong, so she showed up late and was all flustered. Madeline was there in her cast and so was her whole family. It was nice to see her so happy.

The only one who wasn't there was Nammy which surprised me. At first I kept looking out on the street, thinking she would show up. After awhile though, I quit looking. I had too many other things to worry about.

TWENTY-NINE

Ashley Aiken was the first one off the new bus from Franklin. It didn't seem possible but she'd grown since I last saw her. She had always been big, but now she looked like a giant or something. Everyone in our league wore black shoes that you buy down at Comb's Shoe Store. Everyone, that is, except Ashley. She had red leather shoes with black stripes that forced you to stare at them. They were probably specially made because her feet were so enormous. Right away we were all talking about her shoes. This wasn't good for our concentration. But if you get that many teenage girls together and it's the first time they've seen a new shoe, I don't see how anything else could happen.

During warm-ups it was my job to kick the ball out to the team. Ashley couldn't help but see that now I could boot the ball pretty far. But that didn't stop her from giving me one of her sneers. Usually, I looked away, but this time I didn't. I could tell it bothered her.

Otto gave us a longer talk than normal. He said to concentrate and play as a team and pass and communicate and a bunch of other stuff that you hear but don't hear. We'd been told these same things about a thousand times. But we all acted interested because it was Otto. Just watching his mouth move was pretty entertaining.

No one scored early in the game and the teams seemed to be evenly matched. Courtney led a few good drives down to their goal and we took some shots. They could have gone in if the wind had been right or if we'd been lucky. The other team had a couple of chances to score but Shawna was all over the ball. Once she blocked a shot that was so hard it knocked her off her feet. I was worried she was hurt but she got up and was okay.

At halftime there was still no score and Otto told us we needed "a breakaway." He said to wait until they all pushed up and their defenders were way forward. Then we should send someone blowing right by them. We all knew that "someone" was Courtney and she listened and nodded her head. Everyone got the picture to pass to her and let her use her speed.

Unfortunately, I think the coach on the other side was saying the same thing. After halftime they scored on a breakaway led by Ashley and her big red feet. Shawna tried to block the shot but it was just impossible. The kick was perfectly placed in the top left corner right over her head. Falling behind made our team play harder. Soon Courtney scored on a header and we were back to a tie game.

Once the scoring starts sometimes it just breaks some kind of voodoo that's on the field because right away we scored again. We all went crazy jumping up and down because we were ahead two to one. It was Maria Morales who scored, which was great because she's a quiet player. She's one of those solid athletes who does everything right but never shows off.

There was lots of time left and we really shouldn't have been celebrating like that. We let down our guard and they then scored twice in a row. In two minutes, we went from being up by one to being down by one. Shawna didn't look so good and I think the pressure was getting to her.

We were down three-to-two with five minutes left in the game. Courtney got the ball away and scored and we were back to a tie game. It was now three all. At this point all of our stomachs were in knots. We had to score. I guess the pressure was too much for Shawna. I could see her put her hands on her knees and hang her head. I knew right away she was breathing funny. I saw her mom and stepdad pacing on the sidelines. They could tell something was wrong. Shawna's mom started looking in her purse for the inhaler and I told Otto.

Shawna came off the field and I started to put on her goalie shirt. Otto looked at Martha Metzler, who was sitting with Jasmine Assad and Heather Clerkin. I knew what he was thinking. All of them were good athletes and none of them were afraid of the ball. He looked back at me and I stopped putting on the goalie jersey. He was right. Too much was at stake.

But instead he just grinned and yelled for me to get out on the field.

THIRTY

Once I was on the grass Courtney said she promised she'd try to keep them all away. I just nodded because my throat was too constricted to even speak. I looked out at Ashley and caught her eye and she smiled. It was a scary smile, the kind that announced fortune had turned her way. I saw Shawna with the inhaler in her mouth and her head between her knees. It didn't look like she'd be coming to my rescue.

The ref whistled to start play and I could feel our whole team tense up. Everyone on my team, especially our defensive players, looked panicked—like our school was on fire or something. If there's one thing I know, it's fear. And I could really see it in their faces. All the spectators must have felt it too because everyone got to their feet. I was afraid I'd throw up. Otto yelled to the ref for time remaining and he yelled back, four minutes.

I did the math. I only had 240 seconds. It

seemed like an eternity.

It was. But of course, right away, Courtney took her game to a higher level. She stole the ball, just went straight down the field through every defender, and scored. We all went crazy. Everyone was jumping around on top of everyone else and the fans were cheering. I started to get the feeling back in my arms and legs. We were now ahead four-to-three, with about a minute left in the game. All we had to do was keep the ball away from our goal.

That turned out to be impossible. Ashley, looking like a big truck with red wheels, came charging down right at me. I started yelling for everyone to get in there and kick it away. She moved as if she'd mow down anyone who stood in her way. Ashley passed off to another player and now both of them were charging at me. Courtney was over on the far side of the field and she sprinted for Ashley. Now Courtney and Ashley and the ball were all heading right for me. I had my eyes glued to their feet, watching and waiting for the kick. But it didn't come. Instead, Ashley purposely turned inward and ran into Courtney's legs. She made it look as if she had been tripped. She then flew up into the air and landed in a heap on the grass.

Of course the ref blew his whistle, and of course Ashley had drawn the foul. Courtney started yelling that it wasn't her fault, which it wasn't. Otto got so red in the face yelling that I thought he was going to burst. When a foul occurs in the goal box it means only one thing: a penalty kick. It was going to be just me and Ashley battling it out for the game.

Everyone was on their feet. I swear it looked like some of the adults were praying. Jose was shouting something but I couldn't hear. Ashley limped around a little bit as if she'd been injured for life. She looked over at me and grinned. I knew she wanted to make me look like a fool. I wanted to cry because I knew she fell on purpose and because I was afraid of the ball and her kick and the crowd. I was also afraid of clowns. Big trees. Any room that's dark. Thunder. Firecrackers. Cats. Motorcycles. Bees. Snowballs. Most knives. Some forks. Car wash places. Elevators. Hamsters. The guys behind the sushi counter who yell when you come in. Certain shades of purple. Alleys. Sprinkler heads. Any dog bigger than a cat and I already explained about the cats. Men in beards. Men in moustaches. Blood. Ketchup (because it looks like blood). And most kinds of cheese.

And now all of it was in the ball that was placed on the ground. All of it was right in front of me.

But when I looked out, the one thing I wasn't afraid of was Ashley. She had her cool red shoes and her expensive haircut. Her braces had come off before anyone else so she had teeth like in the movies. But I didn't see a whole bunch of people chanting her name or waving their arms. I didn't see hugging and trembling and freaking out because she got to take a shot on me. She wasn't wearing shoes some nice family had bought for her. She probably also didn't have a lucky rock in her right sock.

So I looked her right in the eye. Now I'd noticed something in all those hours I'd spent watching Madeline practice and scrimmage. When players take a shot on goal, they look, for just the smallest of moments, at the spot they're aiming for. They'll look there, just to put it in their brain. Now they may look everywhere else afterwards, but they'd revealed their plan. I watched every twitch of her eyes and for just a flash, just a glance, she looked left.

Ashley pulled her hair back and charged at the ball. As her foot made contact I didn't wait. I forgot about how hard the dirt was and how a ball could hurt you. I forgot about all of the things that make me afraid and I dove left.

THIRTY-ONE

Which doesn't make me a great goalie or anything, but I blocked her shot. And I have to say, when that ball hit my hands, it really, really, really hurt. But I didn't feel it for long because two seconds later the game was over. Everyone was jumping on top of me (which didn't feel that great either), but I was too excited to tell them to get off. Otto ran out onto the field and so did all our players and Shawna's asthma started calming down and the next thing I knew Courtney was hugging me and Jose was out there and all the cool boys, too. It looked like the pictures I've seen of New Year's Eve in big cities where everyone is going nuts.

So we went crazy for awhile and then we sort of calmed down. Otto took us players aside and said that he was so proud of us. Courtney gave us all a look and we said together, "Nagyon szepen koszonom, kocsi." He got tears in his eyes and couldn't speak which made us feel really weird. But then he looked away and coughed and acted like he had a medical problem. Everything was okay.

Me and Courtney said good-bye to everyone about a million times and got in her parents' car. I tried to call Nammy to tell her the good news. It was just like her not to answer. She says the only people who call after dark want to sell her a newspaper subscription or get her to change her long distance telephone service. I whispered to Courtney that I didn't ever remember being as happy. Courtney said she'd never been as happy, too, which I found hard to believe because she's won all kinds of things. But I didn't bring that up.

I was so excited I was singing when I ran to my front door. I opened the door and burst inside calling out for Nammy.

It took me a few seconds to realize it was dark inside which was weird. The TV also wasn't on. I flipped on the lights and I saw right away that the stuff was still out from the chocolate chip pancakes Nammy made in the morning. That wasn't so strange though because sometimes she's not very good about cleaning up. I yelled for her again and went right to her room. I turned on the lights and there she was lying in bed. I started to shout that we'd won but the words got stuck in my mouth. Everything was all wrong. I fell to my knees against the bed and my body went numb. It was as if I was there but I wasn't there all at the same time. I buried my head in the pillows by her hair. The smell of the white face cream she always wore was strong and my hand touched her bare shoulder and it was cold and I knew she had left me.

I realize now that I'd been afraid this would happen my whole life even though I'd never even once thought about it. One day she wouldn't be shuffling around the house singing her songs ever again. And even though my legs were all dirty I climbed up onto the bed to be right next to her. I told her that I loved her and that I didn't want her to go and that I was going to miss her forever and ever and then some more. I said it wasn't fair for her to leave me. I told her that she should have taken me with her. I said she'd been a good Nammy. She'd been a great Nammy. She'd been everything to me.

I don't remember much else about the night. I know I called Courtney, and she and her parents came over. Her mother is a doctor so she knew what to do. I stayed with them for a whole week and didn't go to school or anything.

My Uncle Arnold flew out from back east. There were all kinds of meetings with people but I never went to them. They finally sat me down one day at Izzy's Deli in the red booth in the back. They told me that Nammy had a heart attack and died right away. I think they thought it would make me feel better to hear them say it all together with warm waffles on the table. They said she would have been eighty-six years old, which I didn't know. She was always saying she was younger. I realized then that she slept a lot because she was old, not because she was getting over the flu like she always said.

They gave me a bunch of choices about my life, which was good. They wanted me to be part of what was going to happen. All kinds of people had said they would take care of me. Uncle Arnold offered to take me and not just because by law he had to or something. Even the Bilsessers said I could come live at their house. They'd convert their garage and move the boys there so there would be more room. But I decided I didn't want any of it.

I'd read about a boarding school that was only a few hours away. Kids came there from all around the country and it looked very safe and orderly. What I liked most was that everyone would be on their own just like me. The kids in the pictures didn't look mean and none of them knew me or Nammy or anything about my life, which made me feel better about things. I was afraid to tell Courtney but when I did she didn't get mad. She thought for a long time in silence and then said she wanted to go, too. With Otto leaving, she couldn't take the idea of both of us being gone. Since she couldn't immigrate to Europe, she'd work on her parents for boarding school

I was surprised everybody said yes to our plan. I'd stay with Courtney's family on holidays and I'd see Jose and all my friends. We'd sell Nammy's house so there would be money for me for college. A lawyer was going to be in charge of it until I was older. The boarding school said they had room for me for the last school term. I was going to go up right away, and Courtney would start the next fall.

Everyone was really nice to me when they found out I was leaving. The team had a party for me and Madeline gave me her goalie shirt. Otto came and he sat with us, not the parents, which was so great. He was leaving for Hungary so it was a good-bye party for both of us. Everyone cried at the end and I think it was mostly about saying good-bye to Otto, but I didn't hold that against any of them.

My advisor at school, Mrs. Wiener, got all weepy at the end. She said she'd like to give me something to remember the school by. I said I'd really love to have a library book called "Anomalies of Nature." When she asked why I told her I thought I was an anomaly of nature. After that they didn't have a problem with me taking it.

Ms. Biculos named me as a finalist in the science fair. I think she felt sorry for me because my experiment sucked and everyone knew it. Coach Moshofsky wrote me a recommendation for boarding school and so did Otto. Even Ashley Aiken and her parents dropped off a box of fancy chocolates for me, which just proves that people are gray and not all jerks all the time.

There was only so much stuff I could bring to

the new school. I knew I wanted the trunk with my Mom's stuff for sure. Then a second trunk of things from Nammy, like her black wig and TV changer. But when I went through my own stuff I realized that my soccer shoes and the little medal I got for being on the team meant the most to me. I decided I was going to try and play at the new school. I was glad I could run two miles without really getting tired. Not to mention that I could kick a ball thirty yards.

When I was packing I made a promise to myself. When I got scared I was going to act like I was the keeper. I was going to look for signs of what would happen. Maybe I'd see them. Maybe I wouldn't. But I wasn't going to quit.

My new secret was that I'd seen more than most kids my age. And despite that, I wasn't always going to be afraid.

THIRTY-TWO

In the years that passed I came to love the sport of soccer. In high school, I was captain of the team with Courtney. We were both voted All-League and then All-State in a coaches' poll. I play soccer in college on a full scholarship, which is where I am today.

Courtney lettered in three sports in high school and then surprised us all. She decided to study Slavic History at an excellent university back east. We still speak on the phone once a week and her parents and brothers are my family now, along with a big group of friends who have been there for me for the last eight years. Jose now works at the hospital in the x-ray division. His oldest son is pre-med at the local college. Mr. Hockstatter married Ms. Biculos a few years ago. She's now called Ms. Biculos-Hockstatter, which is really a mouthful.

Soccer has been the most steady and stable thing in my life since eighth grade. I cannot imagine where I would be today without the game. I have now traveled around most of the country playing in matches. I know many of my closest friends because of the sport.

But I will never forget the time when I couldn't kick a ball. Or run for more than a block. I will never forget the person who was afraid of the world. Most of all, I will never forget the team and the people who were there to help that girl. Along with my beloved Nammy, they are always with me every step of the way. They give me strength when I can't see what's in the shadows. And they make it possible for me to live my life in the light.

TEST YOURSELF...ARE YOU A PROFESSIONAL READER?

Chapters 1-3

After reading Chapter 1, what can you interpret about Sasha's friendship with Courtney? Her relationship with Nammy?

Sasha is an expert on scary things. Explain.

Why does Nammy own three automatic cat box cleaners and not even one cat?

ESSAY

Describe the 'ice age' in this book. Have you ever had a similar experience with one of your friends? What did you learn from your 'ice age'?

Chapters 4-6

From what you know about Courtney's personality, would you think she would be successful in the science fair? Use examples from the text to back your choice.

Why did Sasha go along with Courtney's attempt to have her try-out for the basketball team?

Why doesn't Nammy have ice cream in the house anymore?

ESSAY

Did Sasha achieve what she originally planned by trying out for the basketball team? What did she receive? Was Courtney satisfied that Sasha tried out?

Chapters 7-8

What reasons did Sasha give for being afraid of Courtney's older brother, Ned?

Why did Sasha eventually try-out for the soccer team?

What was the one thing that Nammy owned that could possibly be considered an athletic piece of equipment?

ESSAY

Why didn't Sasha want Ashley Aiken to see her shopping at the Salvation Army? Do you think it was right for Ashley to laugh at Sasha when she saw her at the Salvation Army? Explain your answer.

Chapters 9-11

Why did Nammy decide to donate 'stuff' to the Salvation Army?

Who did Sasha blame for Nammy being brought to the police station?

Why does Sasha feel like a spy at soccer tryouts?

ESSAY

Otto's presence brings out the best of Courtney's soccer skills. Name someone in your life that encourages you to excel. Explain why this person is so important to you. Why do you want to do well for this person?

Chapters 12-14

What was the 'only thing that Sasha was good at?'

What sort of "miracle" did Sasha witness on the first day of try-outs?

What was the only sport that Nammy understood? Why?

ESSAY

Sasha broke down the players at tryouts into four groups. Name them. Which group did Sasha place herself into? According to Sasha, which type of player made her want to "scream?"

Chapters 15-17

Sasha had a funny way of showing that she was excited to make the soccer team. How did she show her emotions?

Would Otto have been impressed by Sasha's eating habits? What did her daily breakfast consist of?

Why was Sasha excited when Otto told her that she would be the third string goalie?

ESSAY

What fears caused Sasha to form a plan to change the game of soccer? What did Sasha have in mind on her 'crusade' to change the sport? What did these plans reveal about Sasha's personality?

Chapters 18-20

Was Sasha a big fan of the mystery meat during lunch? Explain.

Will Nammy pretty much eat anything? Explain.

Who was Hilly Saunders? Why did Otto remind Sasha of her?

ESSAY

Sasha says that this is the first time since 'Campfire Girls' that she has been a part of a group. She also claims that 'doing things in a group can make you do way more than you'd do on your own?' Why do you think this is true? Can you think of an example in your life when you did more because you were in a group?

Chapters 21-23

How did Nammy show Sasha that she was excited about her making the soccer team?

What convinced the 'cool guys' to start attending the girls soccer games?

According to Sasha, why was Franklin Middle School a scary place?

ESSAY

What did Otto mean when he said that a player could 'see the field' while they are playing? Explain. Is Courtney one of these special players that can 'see the field'? Is Sasha?

Chapters 24-26

Why was goaltending in direct contrast to Sasha's 'natural instincts?'

Why was Otto impressed by the way in which Sasha tended the goal, even though a shot never came her way during practice? What did her style of goaltending teach the team?

By competing in a sport, Sasha found herself to be a changed person. How did playing soccer change her?

ESSAY

In chapter 27, Sasha says that 'if you tell someone they are something good, they can be more of it.' Name a time in your life when someone gave you a compliment that made you feel better about yourself or a time when you gave someone else a compliment that made them feel better. What do compliments do for self-confidence? Is Sasha affected by Otto's compliments?

Chapters 27-29

What eventually happened to Shawna in Chapter 28 that enabled Sasha to become the starting goalkeeper?

What was the "big surprise" waiting for Sasha on the morning of the game against Franklin?

What does "Nagyon szepen Koszonom, Kosci" mean in Hungarian?

ESSAY

Name at least three of the people who came out to watch the big game against Franklin. Describe Sasha's relationship with each one of them. Who wasn't at the game? If you played in a big game, name three people in your life who would be there.

Chapters 30-32

What clue did Sasha notice in all those hours of shagging balls in practice that helped her make the save on Ashley Aiken's final kick?

When Sasha stepped up to defend that final kick, she was over-coming her fears. Has there ever been a moment in your life when you overcame your fears? Explain.

In the future, what was Sasha going to do to ease her fears when she was afraid of something?

ESSAY

Congratulations! You have completed a Scobre Press book! Now tell us what you learned from Sasha's life, and how you plan on making your own dreams come true.